J. T. EDSON'S
FLOATING OUTFIT

The toughest bunch of Rebels that ever lost a war, they fought for the South, and then for Texas, as the legendary Floating Outfit of "Ole Devil" Hardin's O.D. Connected ranch.

MARK COUNTER was the best-dressed man in the West; always dressed fit-to-kill. BELLE BOYD was as deadly as she was beautiful, with a "Manhattan" model Colt tucked under her long skirts. THE YSABEL KID was Comanche fast and Texas tough. And the most famous of them all was DUSTY FOG, the ex-cavalryman known as the Rio Hondo Gun Wizard.

J. T. Edson has captured all the excitement and adventure of the raw frontier in this magnificent Western series. Turn the page for a complete list of Berkley Floating Outfit titles.

J. T. EDSON'S
FLOATING OUTFIT
WESTERN ADVENTURES
FROM BERKLEY

J.T. Edson

THE MAN FROM TEXAS

BERKLEY BOOKS, NEW YORK

Originally published in Great Britain by Brown Watson Ltd.

This Berkley book contains the complete
text of the original edition.
It has been completely reset in a typeface
designed for easy reading, and was printed
from new film.

THE MAN FROM TEXAS

A Berkley Book / published by arrangement with
Transworld Publishers Ltd.

PRINTING HISTORY
Brown Watson edition published 1965
Corgi edition published 1969
Berkley edition / November 1984

ISBN: 0-425-07307-6

A BERKLEY BOOK® TM 757,375
Berkley Books are published by The Berkley Publishing Group,
200 Madison Avenue, New York, New York 10016.
The name "BERKLEY" and the stylized "B"
with design are trademarks belonging to
Berkley Publishing Corporation.
PRINTED IN THE UNITED STATES OF AMERICA

THE MAN FROM TEXAS

CHAPTER ONE

Take The First Man Through The Door

The town of Goodnight, in the Texas Panhandle country bordering the New Mexico line and north of the
town of Amarilla, lay under a blanket of uneasy silence like the still and calm before a storm. Yet it
was pay day for the local ranches and pay day in
Goodnight usually meant a round of wild excitement
and horseplay as the cowhands, fresh from a month's
work on the range, tried to spend their hard-earned
money in one hectic afternoon, evening and night.

Lines of horses stood hip-shot at the hitching rails
before the saloon, billiard hall, barber's shop, stores
and other business premises, proving that pay had
been made and the cowhands were in town. Yet only
one of the town's businesses had any customers and
even that one did not give out its usual sounds of
cowhand merriment.

The attention of every citizen of Goodnight appeared to be riveted on the large—two story high no
less—imposing front of the Juno Saloon where the
ranchers and their crews foregathered in solemn con-
course to discuss a matter of vital importance. The
business being thrashed out in the Juno Saloon was

1

one which might affect the future well-being and very existence of the town as well as the local ranches. Handled properly, the business could mean prosperity for the area. Mishandled in any way it could ruin the ranchers, or cause such lasting bitterness that trouble and even a ruinous range war might spring from it.

The inside of the Juno Saloon presented an appearance more in keeping with a trail-end city than to a small cow town. Its big barroom had all the latest fittings, a large mirror behind the bar, the bar made of polished wood and with brass foot-rail and spittoons, a small stage on which singers or dancers could perform, or a band play to supply music for public dancing on the small cleared space in the center of the floor. There were tables and chairs where the customers might sit and drink while watching the show; the inevitable tiger-decorated faro layout, chuck-a-luck, black-jack and wheel-of-fortune catered for the sports who preferred gambling to dancing or sitting talking at the tables. Normally a large variety of drinks could be obtained, but on that Saturday afternoon no liquor passed over the bar's shining top.

Around the room, the cowhands stood in groups, or sat at tables. Tall, short, medium-sized; lean, middle-sized or bulky. Yet most had that undefinable something which set the cowhand as a man apart. They wore their hats shaped in much the same manner. Their bandanas ran a glorious riot of every imaginable shade and combination of colors. Gay shirts appeared to be the order of the day, levis pants showed signs of pressing-iron and boots bore an unaccustomed shine; for the men were in town to celebrate and that called for one's best clothes. Almost every man in the room had at least one revolver on his person, but that meant nothing, for a man rarely went unarmed in Texas.

Usually the cowhands in the saloon would have mingled together, drinking, talking, meeting friends from other spreads, making fresh qcquaintances, indulging in good-natured horseplay, flirting with Candy Carde's girls—Candy herself was regarded as being too nice and important a lady to be accorded such easy-going familiarity—or trying to get rich beating the house's percentage on the various games of chance.

Instead of the friendly mingling, the cowhands stood or sat silently in well-defined ranch groups; and silence in those cowchasing Texas sons-of-a-saddle had always been an ominous sign. Every man's attention stayed on the table which had been drawn out into the center of the dance floor, watching the ten men who sat around it. Some of the ten wore expensive clothes which bore testimony to their wealth and social position. Others looked little or no different from the watching cowhands. One of the ten looked like a saddle-tramp. All had one thing in common; they each owned a ranch on the hundreds of square miles of land recently liberated from the Comanches.

On the removal of the Indians, the vacated land had been split up and sold to the ten men around the table. Now it was late March, winter had gone and the time had come for the ranches to think of gathering in their free-ranging stock and checking on the numbers of cattle they owned. To ensure a complete gathering of their long-horned, four-legged harvest it was to their mutual advantage to organize and act in concert. So a meeting had been called to lay plans for a roundup. Naturally such a meeting was held in town; and inevitably Candy Carde's Juno Saloon served as the meeting place.

While every rancher agreed on the benefits of a mass roundup, including an enormous saving of money and time, they failed to agree on the most vital and important issue of all.

Who would be their roundup captain?

On the answer to that vital question rested the success or failure of the venture. The roundup captain ran the whole danged she-bang as boss over all and whose word was law. Nor did the roundup captain's social position affect the issue. He might be the owner of the largest ranch in the area, or a top hand working on a small outfit, but as roundup captain he reigned supreme. It did not matter if he gave orders to a cook's louse or the boss of a large ranch—the two opposite ends of the rangeland social scale—his words must be obeyed. Which meant that not just any man would be suitable.

The roundup captain needed to know cattle, be cognizant with the various brands of the area, know how to send the right number of men to the correct place so as to draw the fullest amount of work possible from all concerned. He had to be able to select the best spots in each section covered by the roundup to gather and hold the cattle for cutting and branding. To get the most out of the men, he would need their respect and mere wealth or social position alone did not give him that. Also he needed to be something of a diplomat if he hoped to keep everybody satisfied that they received fair treatment.

One man at the table would have met with everybody's approval.

Stocky, bearded, well-dressed, Charles Goodnight—the town had been named for him and he bore the honorary title "Colonel"—was a man whose personal integrity and knowledge of all things to do with the cattle industry stood beyond question. He knew the local range, having been one of its earliest pioneers and the man most responsible for moving the Comanches peaceably on to their reservation; and he had the respect of the cowhands. But he had to leave on Monday for Houston to help iron out a tricky matter between the Comanches who had trusted his word and a section of the State Legislature that was trying to wriggle out of the deal. Goodnight could not delay his trip for the four weeks or more the roundup would last.

"How about my foreman?" asked Bunyon of the Barbed B.

"My men won't take orders from no *hombre* who fought for the Union in the War," answered Sanders of the Box S. "I'll take on."

Nobody showed any wild enthusiasm to either offer. Not only Bunyon's foreman fought on the Union side in the War Between the States, Bunyon had ridden as a major in a Yankee cavalry outfit. The War and the recently-ended Reconstruction which followed it were too fresh in Texas memories for a Yankee to be acceptable as roundup captain. Nor was Sanders a better choice, despite the fact that he had been a stout supporter of the Confederacy. At best he tended to be a mite truculent and overbearing, not the kind of man to have sufficient tact to control a large body of high-spirited cowhands who all believed their own particular outfit should come first in everything.

"Are you sure you can't make it, Colonel Charlie?" asked young Greg Haslett of the Rafter H.

"Not a chance, Greg," Goodnight answered regretfully, for he could see the way things were going. "Why not let John Poe handle it. He's been my foreman for ten years and knows this range."

"Him and my foreman's been fussing about a waterhole down on the Village grazing." Meadows of the Flying M growled. "Put Poe in and my boys won't take to it."

Which would mean trouble from the start, for Poe was no man to allow any flouting of his authority and the hands of Goodnight's JA were loyal to their boss and foreman.

"How about Greg here?" asked Naylor of the Lazy N. "He knows the range hereabouts too."

An awkward silence followed the words. Naylor was a slim young man who wore spectacles. While he dressed in cowhand clothes and belted a Colt, he was not range-bred. He was an Easterner who came

West for his health and bought in on one of the smaller ranches. So he had neither the ability nor the desire to be elected roundup captain.

Yet in many ways Naylor's suggestion looked sensible enough. Greg Haslett also owned a small place. However, he was a tophand with cattle and did know the country. Against that was the fact that he had married a saloongirl from the Juno and some of the ranchers—or more particularly their wives—would object to him being in command for that reason. The other men, not ruled by their wives or being more broadminded, did not care about Greg's wife, but doubted if he had the personality to control the cowhands.

"I'll do it if you like," said a mild, friendly voice. "Me or Jesse Evans."

All eyes turned to the speaker. He slouched in his chair at the opposite end of the table to Goodnight; a tall, heavily built man with a bald head and a sunreddened, jovial face. The face was that of a friendly, guileless man who one felt could be trusted with life, wife or wealth. Unless one happened to look at the eyes. They were cold, light blue, calculating and unsmiling. Taken without the face, those eyes would have spelled deceit, trickery and danger. The trouble was that very few people noticed the eyes—until too late.

A cheap woolsey hat sat on the back of the man's bald head, he had a frayed old bandana knotted at his throat. A worn old hickory shirt, battered calf-skin vest, patched levis pants and scuff-heeled ready-made boots completed his outfit, for he did not wear a gun. The latter omission caught the eye first. Only a very few men rode unarmed in the wild range country of Texas.

The speaker looked like a saddle-tramp and was known as the Cattle King. His name, John Chisum; his brand, the Long Rail, a straight line burned from shoulder to rump along the body of his stock.

"You?" Dickens of the Bradded D yelped.

"What's up, Dick?" asked Chisum in his deceptively mild, friendly tones. "Don't you trust me or Jesse?"

"It—It's not that, John," Dickens replied; although his voice implied that Chisum might have guessed the reason for his objections.

Dickens' ranch bordered on Chisum's Long Rail and he knew that people who crossed the Cattle King's path often ran into bad luck; such as having barns and other buildings unaccountably burnt down; stock disappear or die in dubious circumstances; or streams suddenly run dry because of mysterious landslides blocking them on Chisum's property. Not that any of the bad luck could be proved as having happened at the Cattle King's instigation.

Knowing of the "bad luck", the last thing Dickens wanted to do was stir up ill-feeling in Chisum's heart.

However, Dickens saw that none of the other ranchers appeared to be wild with delight, or even mildly pleased, when Chisum offered to burden himself with the onerous duties of roundup captain.

There were too many ugly rumors going around of how Chisum built up his wealth and herds after the War for the ranch owners to show any great eagerness at putting the Cattle King in a position of trust.

While Chisum undoubtedly knew cattle and how to handle men, there was some scepticism among his fellow ranchers on how he would discharge his duties. Sure, having a roundup captain would be an advantage—but happen Chisum was elected to the post, the benefit might be all one way, his.

A good number of the men Chisum hired were what he laughingly called "warriors", picked for their skill with a gun rather than outstanding ability at handling cattle. Backed by his "warriors" Chisum could enforce any rules he made for running the roundup.

It was common knowledge that Chisum had hoped to buy considerably more land than came his way, and as roundup captain he might easily use his authority to drive the smaller ranch owners out of business.

All the time the discussion had been going on, Candy Carde stood by the main batwing doors of the saloon. She seemed to be taking the opportunity to breathe in some good Texas air and looking, with woman's curiosity, to see who came into town by the northbound trail.

She was a beautiful woman, five foot five inches tall; and with blonde hair that hung down below the level of her shoulders, curling under neatly at its ends and parted at the left so that the right side curled down and partially hid one sparkling blue eye. Her nose was well formed and her lips full so as to look almost pouting. Not for Candy Carde the simple, garish knee-length frock of the ordinary saloongirl. She wore a silvery gown which left her shoulders bare and was cut low on her bosom, a rich full mound of flesh that rose over a slender waist. The gown clung like a second skin to her waist and richly curving hips, but slit from hem to thigh to allow her shapely, black stocking-clad legs to show attractively as she moved, or lounged casually yet gracefully by the door.

Candy Carde tended to be something of a mystery woman. Not even her employees knew where she came from or why she decided to settle down and run a saloon in a small cow town. She proved capable, knew the saloon trade, could sing and dance at least as well as most of the professional entertainers who appeared in the Juno and had all the accomplishments of a western hostess. Yet nobody could guess why she came to Goodnight instead of taking her un-doubted talents to the more lucrative trail-end or min-ing cities to the north and west.

That afternoon, on hearing of the urgency of the ranchers' business, Candy had dismissed all her girls, told the gamblers to close their games and shut the bar after allowing each customer to buy only one drink—no man could be expected to talk business until he washed the trail dust out of his throat with one snort. Then Candy stood back and waited for the meeting to end. Only it took a mite longer than anybody expected. Already the sun was going down and the meeting had not reached any decision.

Just as Chisum made, and had rejected, his offer, Candy turned from the door and walked across the room. For an instant her swaying hip movements drew almost every cowhand's eyes from the table. She came to a halt at Chisum's side and smiled around the circle of faces.

"Look, boys," she said, "all this whittle-whanging isn't doing my bank account any good at all. Why not agree to a roundup captain and let me start to take your money?"

One of the many things her customers liked about Candy was the charmingly frank manner in which she regarded them. Some saloon owners acted like they were doing the customers a favor by throwing open their rooms and allowing people in. Not Candy, she stated that she welcomed anybody as long as they spent their money and did not go too far beyond the bounds of polite behavior.

"Riding horses into the barroom is out," she had told her customers when the place first opened. "I get embarrassed at being afoot."

Candy knew the way to handle cowhands.

"We could always let Miss Candy say who's going to run the whole she-bang for us," Chisum remarked.

"Oh no!" Candy interrupted as the other men started to look hopeful. "You boys are all my friends; and, what's more important, paying customers. I'm not being put in the middle that way."

"Come on, Candy," said Washman of the Walking W. "Make the choice."

"You might just as well take the next man through the door," she answered.

"By cracky!" Sanders grunted. "Way I feel, that's what I reckon we ought to do."

"Naw," Chisum objected. "It's too chancy."

Probably if anybody other than Chisum had made the remark, the remainder of the party would have agreed. But all or the majority, took the view that Chisum had an ulterior motive for voting against Candy's suggestion.

"Hell!" barked Bunyon. "It's the only way. I say the next man who comes through that door, if he's a cowhand, is made roundup captain."

"That's pretty risky," Goodnight pointed out. "He may not be a man who can handle the chore."

"We'll be no worse off than we are right now, Charlie," Bunyon objected. "And at least he's not likely to be anybody from this area so's he could be siding any particular spread. I'm for the idea."

"Can't say as how I am," Chisum stated. "But let's do it democratic. Show hands all who's for it."

Once again Chisum's opposition welded most of the men together. Six hands raised immediately then Naylor looked around, shrugged and lifted his right arm into the air. Goodnight, Chisum and Haslett did not vote in favor.

"Seven to three," Sanders announced, throwing a triumphant glance at Chisum and pleased for once the Cattle King had not been given his own way.

"Majority rules," Chisum answered, grinning in his most winning manner. "Come on now, you boys aren't serious, are you?"

"We sure are," Dickens answered and a chorus of affirmative rose from the other pro-Candy Carde's suggestion voters.

For once it appeared that Chisum's charm failed him. The more he objected, the greater grew the other men's determination to carry on with their novel method of choosing a roundup captain.

Word ran quickly around the room and soon every cowhand was aware of the manner in which their roundup captain was to be elected. Like their bosses, most of the cowhands were gambling men and the novelty of the method of selection appealed to their sporting instincts.

"Somebody's coming," one of the cowhands said.

Silence dropped on the room, only the ticking of the clock disturbing it. Hoof beats sounded on the street drawing closer. However, the setting sun shone at such an angle that it struck the front windows of the Juno Saloon and prevented anybody seeing the riders clearly enough to form any opinions. As there was no room at the Juno's hitching rail, the newcomers crossed the street and left their horses at a vacant spot before Mrs. Tappley's hat and gown shop.

Leather creaked as men dismounted, then boots thudded dully on the wheel-rutted dirt surface of the street and boomed woodenly in crossing the sidewalk. Every eye went to the door as four obvious Texas cowhands entered.

A low curse, which none of the others noticed, left Chisum's lips as he stared towards the doorway.

One of the quartet was a veritable giant. Six foot three he stood, if an inch; with golden blond hair under a costly white, low-crowned, wide-brimmed Stetson hat of Texas style. His face was almost classically handsome, yet it was tanned, strong and intelligent, a strong-willed man's face. A scarlet silk bandana was tight rolled and knotted around his throat, trailing long ends down over the made-to-measure tan shirt. His shoulders had a great spread to them and the ample width of the shirt sleeves could not conceal the enormous biceps underneath. From his shoulders, he tapered down to a slim waist and long, powerful legs. The man looked like a Hercules in build, an Adonis in features, something of a dandy by his dress; but still he had the undefinable sign of a top hand to western eyes. The gunbelt around his waist supported a matched brace of ivory butted Colt Cavalry Peacemakers, their seven-and-a-half inch barrels in contoured, fast draw holsters. He looked like a man who could use the Colts, gunbelt and holsters to their best advantage.

There stood a man who could make the roundup captain—but he was not the first of the quartet to enter the room.

The second cowhand stood maybe two inches shorter than the giant. A blond also, he was fast developing into a powerful man. Young, handsome and dressed in good range clothes. though not such a dandy as the giant, he too bore the look of a man who knew cattle. The twin staghorn butted Colt Artillery Peacemakers in the fast-draw holsters hung just right and, unless the signs lied badly, the youngster was unusually adept in their use.

Despite his youth, this one also might have served the ranchers' purpose at a pinch—had he been first to enter the room.

Maybe the third member of the group did not fit in so well; but that was not because of any lack of range savvy. He looked even younger than the second blond and stood an inch shorter, but had a lean, wiry, whipcord strength about him. His hair was black as the wing of a deep south crow, yet curly as no Indian hair ever was. Yet there was something Indian about him. It might have been the darkness of the almost babyishly young, innocent-seeming, handsome face or in the red-hazel eyes which were neither young nor innocent. All his clothing was black, from hat down to boots, even the leather of the gunbelt had the same sober hue. Only the ivory hilt of the bowie knife sheathed at his left side and brown walnut grips of the old Dragoon Colt holstered butt forward at his right relieved the blackness.

If the Indian-dark youngster could not make it as roundup captain, it would be inexperience in practical cattle-work which failed him. However, the matter did not arise, for he was the last of the four to enter.

What then did the first man through the door look like?

For a start, he was a small man not more than five foot six in height; although he was not weedily-built. Come to a point, for his size he had a physical development which equalled that of the blond giant. Yet he seemed to fade to nothing compared with any of his friends. It was not as a result of wearing poor clothes. His black Texas-style Stetson, bandana, shirt and levis were all expensive, but he did not have the flair for showing them off as did his friends. He was handsome, though not in an eye-catching manner, yet he had a strong face happen one thought to give him a second glance. His boots bore the look of being made by a master craftsman. So did his gunbelt. Yet the gunbelt, even though hanging correctly, and the matched brace of bone-handled Colt Civilian Peacemakers butt forward for a cross-hand draw, did nothing to make the small man noticeable.

In fact the only reason any of the crowd noticed him at all was because he led the quartet into the room—and was the first man to enter since the ranchers announced how they would elect their roundup captain.

CHAPTER TWO

That There Is Dusty Fog

Although he had been one of the stoutest advocates of the unusual method of selection, Bunyon now felt considerable doubts as he saw the consequences of the idea. He glanced at the small man who entered first, then turned to Goodnight.

"Hell, Charlie," he said. "That short-growed runt'll never make us a roundup captain."

"You go tell him," Goodnight replied, looking more relieved than he had since the idea was put forward. "Tell him you reckon his height'll stop him being able to handle it—only I don't envy you none."

"Do you know him, Charlie?" Sanders asked, watching the four men walk towards the bar.

"You might say that. I stood godfather for him. He rode as my segundo on the third trail drive I made after the War—"

"You're funning us," Bunyon interrupted.

It was the only acceptable way of calling a man like Colonel Charlie Goodnight a lair and living to think twice about the words. Bunyon's incredulity sprouted from his knowledge the name of the man who rode segundo for Goodnight on that historic third

14

trail drive after the War.* And that name could not belong to such a short-growed—

"So I'm funning you," Goodnight grunted. "But that there is Dusty Fog."

With that Goodnight thrust back his chair and rose to his feet. Talk rolled up from the men at the table and all stared at the small, insignificant Texan who had become a legend already in his young life.

In the War folks spoke of Dusty Fog as the seventeen year old commander of Troop "C" of the Texas Light Cavalry and a military raider equal to Turner Ashby or John Singleton Mosby and a thorn in the Yankee army's side until the meeting at the Appomattox Court House brought peace, or a cessation of military action, to the land. Since then Dusty Fog's name had become known as a cowhand of the first water, trail boss, segundo of the great OD Connected ranch and town-taming lawman. In the annals of western gun play he stood second to no man, and many claimed him to be the fastest of them all.

This then was the first man to enter the Juno Saloon after the decision to follow Candy Carde's suggestion had been made.

The handsome blond giant also carried a name. In the War Mark Counter had become known as the Beau Brummel of the Confederate cavalry. Now his taste in clothes for the most part dictated what the well-dressed Texas cowhand wore. His strength was a legend, his skill in a rough-house brawl something once seen never forgotten. If anything, Mark was better with cattle even than Dusty Fog; and might have owned his own ranch, for an aunt left him her considerable fortune when she died, or taken on as foreman of any big spread. But Mark stayed on at the OD Connected, working as a member of the elite of Ole Devil Hardin's crew, the floating outfit. While men knew much about

*Told in: *From Hide and Horn.*

Mark Counter, there were few who could speak with authority of his skill with a gun. He lived under the shadow of the Rio Hondo gun wizard, but those who *knew* claimed Mark to be second only to Dusty Fog in the matter of speed and accuracy.

The black-dressed, baby-faced young man had been christened—or named, for no preacher officiated at the ceremony and no parish record bore mention of his birth—Loncey Dalton Ysabel. Folks mostly knew him as the Ysabel Kid. While the Kid did not claim to be in the same magic-handed class as his three friends, he could handle his old Dragoon with fair skill. However, there were few to equal his mastery of the gentle art of knife-fighting; and he claimed no peer with the magnificent "One of a Thousand" Winchester Model of 1873 rifle he won at the Cochise County Fair.* He was a master of the business of riding scout and could move through the thickest, driest brush in a silent manner that would turn a buck Apache green with envy. At tracking he could claim to be an expert, able to follow the most difficult line. His father had been a wild Irish-Kentuckian, his mother a beautiful Comanche-French Creole girl. From out of the mixing of fighting bloods came a deadly young man. A damned good friend, but a bad mean enemy.

Of all the quartet, the last one was least known, though fast making up for his lack of fame. Left an orphan almost from birth, he bore only one name. Waco. When Dusty Fog first met him, Waco had been riding as part of Clay Allison's wild-onion crew; a trigger-fast-and-up-from-Texas kid with a log-sized chip on his shoulder and a belly-full of suspicion and mistrust towards his fellow men. Dusty had saved Waco's life that day.† Since then Waco followed the Rio Hondo gun wizard with doglike devotion, giving

*Told in *Gun Wizard*.
†Told in *Trigger Fast*.

him the hero-worship and devotion that might have gone to the long dead father. Waco changed from a proddy kid to a useful member of rangeland society. Each of his three friends treated him as a younger brother and taught him all they could.

"Howdy, Uncle Charlie," said Dusty Fog, changing direction as Goodnight walked towards him and giving Bunyon confirmation of Goodnight's words. "I thought my pants were on fire, way everybody stared when I came in."

"Never was more pleased to see a man, Dusty," Goodnight replied, taking the offered hand in a firm grip. "You aren't hide-bound for any place, are you, boy?"

"Only back to home."

"Reckon Ole Devil could spare you for three, four weeks?"

"If it's important enough," Dusty replied and glanced at his friends who had halted and stood waiting for him. "Go get the drinks in, Lon, it's long gone time you bought."

"Don't approve of Injuns drinking," grunted the Kid. "Especially when it's me has to do the paying."

"Just get the three and set back to watch us white folks drinking then," Waco suggested, looking towards the bar and ogling Candy Carde with frank, open-eyed juvenile admiration.

The three cowhands left their leader and made for the bar. Dusty looked at his uncle, then towards the group of men he recognized as being ranch owners who rose and gathered round him. For their parts, nine out of the ten could hardly believe their good fortune at having the famous Dusty Fog walk in at such a moment.

"We'd like you to be our roundup captain, Cap'n Fog," Sanders said and most of the others rumbled their agreement.

"Are they on the level, Uncle Charlie?"

"Sure are, Dustine."

"And *you're* here?"

"I'll explain about things in a couple of minutes, boy," Goodnight answered, pleased with the compliment Dusty paid to his ability as a cattleman. "Sure like you for to accept, though."

"Then I'm on—if you'll be the one who explains to Uncle Devil how come I've been delayed."

"I'll see to it," Goodnight promised with a grin.

He could visualize Ole Devil's reaction to the news that the OD Connected's segundo and three best hands would be four weeks late arriving home. It would be worth money to hear the irascible old rancher's comments. Not that Ole Devil would really object, but he liked to have an excuse to sharpen his horns and start pawing the dirt.

"You'll do it then, Cap'n?" Bunyon inquired, forgetting his original misgivings at taking such a small, insignificant man on as roundup captain.

"He'll do it," Goodnight agreed.

Instantly talk welled up around the room. There had been some surprised comment and disappointment when Dusty entered. The hands who did not know him could not see themselves taking orders from such a small feller. Now Dusty's name bounced from mouth to mouth and all knew that they had truly got a roundup captain.

"Can't think of a better man for the chore, Cap'n," Chisum said, stepping forward. "Of course there's some it might not suit so well."

"World'd be a helluva place happen we all liked the same things, Mr. Chisum," Dusty replied.

"Reckon it would at that," agreed Chisum, ignoring the knowledge that a Texan never used the word "mister" after being introduced unless he did not like the man he called it.

Turning, Chisum walked away. He headed towards the door and a nod of his head brought three of his hard-case crew after him. None of the other ranchers saw him go, for all were talking to Dusty Fog.

"When do we start, Captain?" Naylor asked.

"Whose range'll you be working first?" Washman went on.

"What do we do about dough-guts?" put in Bunyon before Dusty could answer any of the questions.

"Hold on there!" Goodnight boomed. "Back off a spell. Let me have a talk with Dustine, set him wise to the lay of the land afore you start working on the circle and cutting the herd."

"That's fair enough," Haslett agreed. "Come on, fellers, I'll set up the first round."

Haslett led the other ranchers to the bar where Candy's bartenders were already to work. After they went, Goodnight nodded to a side table and suggested he and his nephew took the weight off their feet.

"What's all this about, Uncle Charlie?" Dusty asked, sitting down.

Quickly Goodnight explained about the roundup, and the conditions which brought about the unusual method of selecting their leader. Mark, the Kid and Waco had gathered at the table, bringing beers for Dusty and Goodnight, and sat listening. Although he had once been Chisum's friend,* Goodnight did not hide his suspicions of the Cattle King's motives and aspirations.

The mention of Chisum's name caused the Kid to glance around the room in search of the Cattle King. He saw Chisum return to the barroom, followed by the three hard-cases, head for the bar and buy a bottle of whisky which he handed to one of the trio. Knowing Chisum to be tight-fisted, the Kid wondered at the unexpected burst of generosity. Being a suspicious and watchful young man by nature, the Kid kept his eyes on the three men, especially as they walked for-

---

*Why the friendship ended is told in *Goodnight's Dream*.

ward and sat at the next table to his own.

"Hey, just look at who's come in!"

Mark's soft-drawled words brought all the occupants of the table's eyes to the front door of the saloon. Half-a-dozen gun-hung men entered and stood for a moment looking around them with quiet, watchful gaze. They wore cowhand style clothes, only of a better cut than most cowhands could afford. In the lead, and first to enter, was a tall, slim young man with a smiling face that showed buck teeth. He wore a black Stetson with a silver concha decorated band around it, a dark blue shirt, black levis and boots, while a gunbelt around his waist supported matching pearl-handled Civilian Model Colts.

"Know them, Dusty?" Goodnight asked.

For a moment Dusty studied the newcomers, then he nodded. "That's Billy Bonney in the lead. What's he doing here, do you reckon?"

"Not what," growled Goodnight. "Who."

Watching the young man soon to become famous as Billy the Kid, Dusty got the impression that Bonney had been expecting a different reception. One of the men behind Bonney growled something and the bucktoothed youngster grinned over his shoulder, then walked across the room to where Chisum sat alone at the opposite side to Goodnight's party.

"I'd sure like to know what's being said over there," Goodnight remarked as Bonney sat at Chisum's table and poured a drink from the Cattle King's bottle-neck down his throat and then started speaking.

The conversation between Chisum and Bonney would have been both interesting and enlightening to Goodnight, but unfortunately for him, he did not hear it.

"What went wrong, Uncle John?" Bonney asked, using Chisum's pet name.

"Where've you been?" Chisum asked, in as near a growl of anger as he dare use with the smiling young killer.

"That's a right sweet lil daughter your Mexican cook's got," Bonney answered. "I got to—talking with her, and you know how time does fly. When they going to start electing me round-up captain?"

"They aren't."

"Aren't, huh?" A hard note crept into Bonney's voice.

"You came too late. Another feller walked in through the door."

"Did, huh?"

"Sure. He got elected, too."

"Now that's a thing's can soon be altered. Where's he at?"

"There, the short runt sat talking with Goodnight."

Slowly and casually Bonney turned in his seat, as if looking around the room for old friends. In passing he meant to study the man who had taken what he had hoped would be a well-paid job for a deserving young feller like William Bonney. On his eyes reaching Goodnight's table, Bonney stiffened slightly and swung back towards Chisum.

"You wouldn't be playing all sneaky and tricky, now would you, Uncle John?" he asked, his eyes alight with suspicion.

"What d'you mean, Billy?"

"That there's Dusty Fog."

"Have I denied it?"

"Nope. But you didn't mention it none, either. If I thought this was a piece of your tricky—"

"So help me, Billy, why would I be tricky with you?"

"Maybe to keep your hand in," Bonney spat out.

"Look, I sent for you in good faith. Only things went wrong. There's one sure way you could still be roundup captain."

"My mother didn't raise any half-witted children, *Mr.* Chisum. I'm not fixing to stack up against Dusty Fog, not when he's got those three fellers backing him. That's being understood, if you'll pay me off

I'll be riding back to New Mexico and taking my boys along."

"Paying you—?" Chisum began.

"Maybe you'd like me to tell folks about your lil plan to have me made roundup captain?"

A worried expression flitted across Chisum's face. He knew what would happen if word of his planned deception got out. Not even their old friendship would stop Goodnight taking action, and only Goodnight prevented the other ranchers from banding together and driving Long Rail from their midst.

"I was only joking, Billy. You're a good boy; and it's a mortal sin that you should be d—"

"Don't try it, Chisum. You can't talk me into stacking against him."

"I'll have the money for you as soon as you like," Chisum growled.

"Now's as good a time as any," Bonney replied.

"Not in here!" Chisum protested. "Look around—"

"Plenty of room outside. Let's go."

Reluctantly Chisum rose and followed Bonney out of the saloon. Bonney's gang left on their boss's heels, for they knew they were not welcome in the Texas Panhandle. While Bill Bonney's men might be tough and dishonest, they were not stupid. There were men in that room as tough and handy with guns as any of them; and being wise outlaws, they did not aim to outstay their welcome.

After paying Bonney off, the Cattle King watched the young outlaw ride out of Goodnight with the gang on his flanks. Chisum felt fury boil up inside him at the failure of his plan and what he regarded as Bonney's cowardice. However, like a wise general, he had arranged for a second line of attack. Maybe that one would work. Turning, Chisum returned to the saloon to see if the second string to his bow would prove any stronger than his first.

In the saloon Candy Carde watched and listened to the usual pay day revels starting up. She smiled as she saw Chisum's departure with Bonney, then her smile faded a little and lines of worry creased her brow. While she had done her part as ordered, things appeared to have gone wrong and she might be blamed for the mistake. Her eyes happened to glance at Goodnight's table as the thought came to her and she studied the four men around it. While not being range-bred, Candy had heard the names of Dusty Fog, Mark Counter, the Ysabel Kid and, to a lesser extent, Waco, often enough to know something of them. All had the name for being loyal to their friends. The way Candy looked at it, she needed somebody like that on her side—and had for the past two years.

With Candy to make a decision was to act on it. She crossed the room, smiling a welcome to the other guests and passing the three Long-Rail hardcases' table. Glancing at the men she saw they were punishing a bottle of her best whisky and remembered Chisum presenting them with it. Like the Kid, Candy had no illusions about Chisum's generosity. If the Cattle King handed three of his men a bottle of whisky, he aimed to get a good return for his money.

"I don't reckon we should have a roundup captain just 'cause he's reckoned to be a fast gun!" the big, curly haired, dark faced tough at the side farthest away from Goodnight's party announced in a carrying voice.

Candy had an instinct for trouble. In her time around saloons, she had learned how to read the signs. Those three hard-cases were trying to spark something off, and, unless Candy mistook the signs, they aimed to start it with Dusty Fog.

"Have you finished talking business, Colonel Charlie?" she asked, coming up to Goodnight's table. "If so, how about introducing me to your guests?"

All the Texans thrust back their chairs and came to their feet in a polite manner. Goodnight introduced Mark, Waco and the Kid, then said, "This's my nephew, Captain Dustine Edward Marsden Fog, Candy. Dustine, meet our lady saloon-keeper, Miss Candy Carde."

"My pleasure, ma'am," Dusty replied, taking the girl's offered hand.

A nasty snigger came from the next table and the thin man seated with his back to the wall said, "My, ain't he the cute one, Curly?"

"Sure is," the biggest of them replied. "I do declare, he's a southern gentleman for sure."

"Now me," the third announced. "I likes a boss who's a man not a fast gun gentleman."

"Easy, boy!" Dusty ordered as Waco started to turn from the table. "Sit down, we'll tend to their needings later."

Candy looked at Dusty with fresh interest. Never again would she think of him as being small. Somehow, as he spoke, Dusty put on inches, took on size until he stood the tallest of them all. Candy's plans made a sudden change. From planning to make herself pleasant to Mark Counter, she changed her aim and decided Dusty Fog might better suit her purpose.

"May I join you, Captain Fog?" she asked.

"It'd be our pleasure, Miss Carde," Dusty replied, then smiled as he drew out a chair for her. "Only folks old enough to be my grandfather call me Dustine, and 'Captain's' a mite formal."

"I think Dustine is a charming name," she answered, waving the men into their seats. "Can we dispense with the prefixes, Dustine?"

"My, Dustine, ain't that sweet?" sniggered the big man in a voice loud enough to carry to the nearby tables.

Once more Dusty stopped Waco rising and going to the hard-cases' table. Yet Dusty knew a clash must come, the three men seemed determined to start one. They were drinking, which might be an excuse for their behavior and Dusty took no pleasure in teaching drunks the error of their ways.

"Who are they, Colonel?" asked the Kid.

"Big one calls himself Curly, allows to be some hard citizen. Skinny feller with his back to the wall is Gordon and the narrow one with his back to us goes by the name of Walker. They ride for Long Rail."

"And they're drinking Mr. Chisum's liquor," Candy remarked, then looked at Dusty. "So you're to be roundup captain, Dustine."

"So they tell me."

"It was Candy who started the idea of us taking the first man through the door," Goodnight said. "The boys couldn't agree and she suggested it.

"I only said it as a joke," she corrected, "but the boys took me seriously. Although looking at it now, the way it turned out I should pretend I knew all along it was the best idea for selecting the roundup captain."

"Would you care for a drink, Candy?" Dusty asked.

"Not on an empty stomach," she replied.

"Which same reminds me, Dusty," Waco drawled, eyeing the three hard-cases hopefully. "I'm hungry."

"Day you're not'll be the change," Mark drawled, watching Candy with calculating and interested eyes. "Do you serve food here, Candy?"

"I'm afraid not, Mark."

"We'll have to get him fed. Boy's mean and ornery any time. But he's a danged sight worse when he's not been fed. Coming Lon, Dusty?"

"That depends on where we have to go to eat," Dusty replied.

"Widow Bauman's café along Main Street is the best place in town," Candy put in. "In fact that's where I go when I eat."

"And when's that?" Dusty asked.

"If a gentleman was to ask, I'd say as soon as I've changed into something more suitable for wearing outside."

"That lets you bunch out," grunted the Kid. "Ain't

but the one gentleman here, Miss Candy."

"Oh, I don't know," she replied. "Mark and possibly Waco, when he gets a little older, might qualify, don't you think Dusty?"

"If they do," he answered. "I'll be tolerable surprised. Shall we say in fifteen minutes, Candy?"

"Make it twenty. I'm a woman, don't forget."

"A man'd need to be dead before he forgot *that,*" Dusty said. "Twenty minutes, then."

Mark, the Kid and Waco exchanged glances and grins. Give him his due, old Dusty might not go for chasing the gals as much as some who could be named. But once he started, he could sure show a clean and handy pair of heels.

For his part, Goodnight felt slightly disturbed. While he was all for a young feller showing an appreciation for and interest in a pretty gal, he thought maybe Dusty was building difficulties for himself by showing himself too friendly with Candy Carde. Goodnight did not object. But some of the good ladies might not approve of the roundup captain becoming involved with one who they, in their intolerant manner, branded as a scarlet woman.

CHAPTER THREE

Captain Fog Shows His Fangs

Smiling at Dusty's compliment, Candy Carde rose and turned from the table. To get to the stairs leading to her rooms on the upper floor, Candy had to pass the table where the Long Rail men sat. She did not give the men a second thought, except to decide she might be saving them some grief by taking Dusty away before they really annoyed him.

Just as Candy passed, the man called Curly twisted in his chair, raised his foot and stamped the heel down on the trailing hem of her dress. Only just in time Candy stopped, the dress's lower reaches dragging back and exposing her shapley legs. A silence that could almost be felt dropped over the room, for nobody had expected such a liberty to be taken with the owner of the Juno Saloon. At the bar, Candy's two bouncers caught the bartender's signal and turned. They were big men, capable and knew their work. Yet they hesitated an instant before moving in on the Long Rail men.

Candy moved back a pace, turning to look down at Curly with an expression of anger and loathing on her face.

"Move your foot!" she hissed.

Shooting out his hand, Curly caught her by the wrist and pulled her towards him, directing a leer at Dusty Fog. Across the room, a bunch of Long Rail hands, having seen the signs, blocked the path of the bouncers.

"You come on here, Candy gal," Curly said. "You don't want no gentleman to take you to dinner, even if he is supposed to be the roundup captain."

All the men at Goodnight's table had tensed when Curly stopped the girl. Every eye in the room went to Dusty Fog. In the face of what had happened, every man and woman in the room knew Curly's reactions to be an open challenge to the small Texan. The cowhands looked interested, waiting to see how the man whose orders they were expected to obey would handle the situation. If Dusty failed to meet the challenge, he would have no control over the men.

"Let me take him, Dusty," Mark said hopefully; athough he knew Dusty must take up the challenge. "He's my size."

The words carried around the room, so did Dusty's answer.

"Sure, Mark. But I'm *his* size."

Eager expectancy filled the air as Dusty Fog came to his feet. The ranch owners, cowhands and saloon workers waited and watched Dusty. How would he handle the matter? Most likely, in view of his reputation, with his guns, thought the crowd. Well that would be something to see. Curly reckoned to be better than fair with his Colt and it might be interesting to see how he, a Kansas man, stacked up against the fastest gun in Texas.

In that the onlookers were to be disappointed. Fast with his guns though he could claim to be, Dusty was not a killer in the accepted western sense of the word. Every man who had died before his Colts needed killing and died so that Dusty or some other person might live.

Anyway there was a much better way of handling the matter than with a bullet. Dusty knew that shooting Curly would only lead to further trouble with the Long Rail crew. Not for friendship with Curly, but to prove that Long Rail was a wild-onion crew it did not pay to cross. While Dusty did not fear the Long Rail crew individually or as a bunch, he knew gun-trouble on the roundup would interfere with the work, stir up the cowhands and prevent him from satisfactorily carrying out his duty as roundup captain.

No, Dusty did not aim to use his guns when dealing with Curly. Not when he knew a far more effective method of handling the situation. One which would provide a salutary lesson not only to Curly but to the rest of the men who were to work on the roundup under Dusty's orders.

"Let loose!" Dusty ordered, walking forward.

Curly thrust Candy to one side, releasing her wrist. Staggering, the girl came to a halt, being helped by the shot-out hand of one of a group of cowhands sharing a bottle of whisky at a table. Being wise in such matters, Candy did not attempt to go back, but stood by the table out of the way so as not to impede Dusty in any action he took. She felt afraid and sick in her stomach, for she had never seen a man die by violence, although she saw one who had met a violent end shortly after his death.

"I'm not stacking against you with a gun, Fog," Curly stated in a loud and carrying voice.

A neat move on Curly's part. Nobody would blame a man for avoiding facing the Rio Hondo gun wizard with a gun. So, when the Texan declined to handle the matter any other way, Curly, would have made his point. The cowhands were not likely to take orders from a man who relied on his guns to push the orders through.

"Call it any way you like," Dusty replied, his matched Colts flicking out and to his grasp.

For an instant the crowd thought Dusty intended

to cut down Curly in cold blood. So did the Long Rail man if his face's expression did not lie. Turning his back on Curly, Dusty tossed the guns to where Mark sat waiting to catch them. Every member of the crowd stared and a low murmur ran through the room. In tossing aside his guns like that, Dusty accepted Curly's challenge. On the face of it, while they admired his courage, the crowd thought Dusty did not show real good sense in his actions, for Curly was both inches taller and many pounds heavier than the small Texan.

Curly clearly thought he had the edge. Thrusting back his chair, he started to rise, his hand going to the neck of the bottle on the table and his eyes fixed on the back of Dusty's head. He almost made it. Almost, but not quite; and they do say a miss is as good as a mile.

Swinging around, Dusty drove out his left hand. He stepped forward with the punch so as to give Curly the full benefit of it. With the power of a knobhead mule's kick, Dusty sank his left fist almost wrist deep in Curly's unprotected belly. Taken completely by surprise with the force at which the blow landed, Curly let out a strangled squawk and went backwards a few steps, just missing the chair he had thrown over as he rose. Holding his middle, his whiskery face turning a hideous shade of greyish-green, Curly sank to his knees.

Once more the sound of a chair clattering over brought Dusty around to meet another menace to his well-being. Walker had seen Curly go down and looked like he aimed to get into the act. Seeing Dusty's left hand draw back as it had done before ripping into Curly's belly, Walker drew his own stomach in. Doing so stuck his chin out and tilted his head back in a manner that was tempting providence. Dusty took over instead of providence. Most folks would have whipped a punch up under the offered jaw, but the small Texan knew a better way of handling Walker.

Down in the Rio Hondo, Ole Devil Hardin had a small servant thought to be Chinese, but who claimed to have come to America with Commodore J. C. Perry, U.S. Navy, from some place called Japan. Wherever he came from, Tommy Okasi sure knew how to take care of himself. To Dusty, smallest of the Rio Hondo boys, Tommy Okasi taught the secrets of ju-jitsu and karate which made him so deadly. As in most things, Dusty proved an apt pupil—as he proceeded to demonstrate.

Dusty's right hand lashed up, fingers extended, thumb bent across his palm. Like the edge of an axe biting into kindling wood, the side of Dusty's palm chopped across Walker's prominent adam's apple. Walker reeled backwards, clutching at his throat and gagging. While he considered the method of attack highly unsporting, Walker was too busy trying to breathe for him to raise any objections.

Which left Gordon to uphold the proud name and great traditions of the Long Rail. Not that he brought off anything spectacular in his try at showing the small Texan who was boss. In all fairness, however, it must be said of Gordon that he never expected his services would be needed to handle one small man. When it dawned on him that Curly and Walker had both failed, he realized that he must do something to earn his share of the boss's bottle of whisky. So he started to thrust his chair back ready to rise.

Turning, Dusty raised his right foot and shoved the table violently into Gordon. The Long Rail man's right hand had just clamped on its gun butt when the edge of the table drove into his belly and pinned him against the wall. Giving a yelp of pain, Gordon forgot about drawing his gun. Lowering his leg, Dusty shot both hands across the table. He clamped a hold of the front of Gordon's vest and shirt, hauling the man forward across the top of the table. As Dusty expected, Gordon strained the other way in an attempt to stop himself joining Dusty. Releasing his hold suddenly, Dusty brought his right fist whipping across. The result looked highly spectacular. Due to the strength of his pull, Gordon was already off balance and starting to go backwards when Dusty hit him. So the man shot away even faster than the blow would have propelled him, hit the wall and hung there for a glassy-eyed moment, then slid down to the floor.

Behind Dusty, Curly was still on his knees. Clutching his middle with his left hand, the man dropped his right towards the butt of his gun. Dusty's attention was fully occupied in handling Gordon his needings so the small Texan did not realize his danger.

Mark had laid Dusty's guns on the table top as soon as he caught them, then turned to watch his friend in action. Now he, Waco and the Kid saw Dusty's danger and prepared to act. Fast movers though the trio were, Candy Carde showed even greater speed and just as quick a grasp of the situation. Her hand shot out and closed on the neck of the bottle of whiskey which stood on the table at her side. It may have been that she decided to follow Curly's example, or just that she grabbed for the first likely weapon which came to hand. Whatever the reason, Candy gripped the bottle and moved forward fast. Swinging up the bottle, she brought it down in a whistling arc towards Curly's head. The bottle crashed down, shattering, spraying broken glass and the remains of the whisky out like a bursting bomb. Luckily for Curly, he had never learned the gentlemanly habit of removing his hat in the presence of a lady. If the bottle had burst on his unprotected head, Curly might never have walked out of the saloon. Even cushioned by his hat, the blow pitched him forward unconscious on to his face.

Hearing the crash, Dusty thrust himself away from the table behind which Gordon slumped, and turned to face the sound. Although he turned prepared for offensive or defensive action, Dusty found he would need to do neither. From the rag-doll limp way Curly, dripping bits of broken glass and with whisky running down his face, fell forward, Dusty did not think he would be getting up for quite a spell.

A momentary silence fell over the saloon as everybody stared at the three defeated Long Rail men. True, Captain Fog had only settled two of them by his own efforts, but nobody blamed Candy for her actions; or doubted that Dusty could have handled Curly by himself. Anyway, Curly called for a fight with bare hands and had no right to grab for a gun when things started to go the wrong way.

"Here endeth the first lesson," Mark drawled, picking up Dusty's guns so as to return them to their owner.

"I surely hope ole Dusty hasn't hurt them too bad," remarked the Kid in a voice which showed a remarkable lack of concern for the welfare of the Long Rail hard-cases.

"Why'n't Dusty cut us in on them three fellers?" asked Waco in annoyance. "I tell you, old Dusty's getting to be a right hawg with his fights."

Candy looked at the broken bottle in her hand, glanced down at Curly, and then lifted her eyes to Dusty's face. For a moment they looked at each other, oblivious of the rest of the room. Giving almost a visible start, Candy brought her old smile to her face, turned and waved forward her bouncers and a swamper.

"Get them out of here," she ordered the bouncers, waving a hand to the defeated Long Rail crew. "Charlie, clear up this mess and tell one of the waiters to bring these Bradded D boys a fresh bottle, they had an accident with the last."

After seeing her orders obeyed, Candy turned to Dusty once more. He pointed to Walker who looked a mite black in the face.

"You'd best get him to the doctor, he isn't breathing too good."

"Curly doesn't look any too happy with things either," Candy replied. "Take them to Doc Baxter's place, boys. You know, Dustine, we make quite a team. You set them up and I knock them down."

"Why, sure," he agreed.

"You said twenty minutes, didn't you?"

"It's nearer fifteen now."

"Then I'd better fly. But remember it's a woman's privilege to be late."

After Candy left his side, Dusty looked around the room. From the expressions on the ranchers' and cowhands' faces, Dusty did not reckon he would have any further objections to his taking the post of roundup captain.

The cowhands regarded Dusty with frank admiration and hero-worship on their faces. Not only had Dusty whipped three Long Rail hard-cases, all bigger and heavier than himself, but he was also taking Miss Candy out for a meal; and she looked at Dusty in a manner they had never seen her show any other man. Yes siree, Bob, that Captain Fog sure was a real big man.

Whatever doubts might have remained in some of the ranchers' minds at hiring a famous gunfighter for their roundup captain were now gone. The fear that they could be hiring a man who relied on speed with a gun to offset his lack of inches and as a means to enforce his will had crossed some minds. Now they knew that Dusty did not need his guns when dealing with awkward men, but carried a right convincing argument in his bare hands.

Lastly the Long Rail crew had learned a lesson they would not soon forget. Curly, Gordon and Walker all reckoned to be hard citizens drunk or sober, yet the small Texan softened their hardness without any great straining of his milk. The men of Long Rail had expected guns to roar, probably more than the others in the room, for they lived by the gun. When Dusty Fog accepted Curly's challenge and shed the guns, Long Rail figured he was making a grandstand play and that Mark Counter or that kid Waco would cut in to help. Only Dusty Fog had not needed any help. Curly and his two pards had been licked. Maybe the next men to try it out on Dusty Fog would not come off so easy.

Talk rumbled up around the room as men eagerly described what they had seen. Dusty returned to his friends and holstered the matched guns. Dropping a wink to Goodnight, he walked across the room to where Chisum sat alone.

"Sorry I had to do that, Mr. Chisum," he said and silence dropped on the room once more.

"Curly and the boys asked for it," Chisum replied, making the only remark he could under the circumstances.

"Miss Carde stopped Curly pulling a gun on me."

"He hadn't ought to have done that."

"He knows it now. Only he looked like the kind who might try to go for evens."

"So?" Chisum asked.

"So this, Mr. Chisum," Dusty replied in a voice which carried around the room. "I am relying on you to make him understand something. If anything, any little thing at all, happens to Miss Carde, I'm holding him responsible."

What Dusty meant, and both he and Chisum knew it, was that he held the Cattle King responsible.

"I understand, Cap'n Fog."

"Yes, sir, Mr. Chisum," Dusty drawled. "I reckon you do at that."

Turning, Dusty walked back to Goodnight's table. If looks could have killed, Dusty would have been a dead man before he took two steps away from the Cattle King's presence.

"Colonel Charlie says we can bunk down at his town house for the night, Dusty," Mark said as Dusty returned. "He's gone to tell John Poe to take us along. We'll collect your paint and tend to it while you get to know the ranchers. Meet you at Widow Bauman's Café later, if you like."

"I'll be there," Dusty replied.

John Poe, Goodnight's tall, tough and efficient foreman, came over to greet Dusty, then escorted the other three OD Connected men from the saloon. Seeing that Goodnight appeared to have settled the details with his nephew, the other ranchers attracted the attention of their foremen and moved it to become acquainted with the man who would rule their lives for the next four or so weeks and on whose ability depended the success of their roundup.

While Goodnight started to perform the introductions, Dusty took the opportunity to study the men. He would need a number of lieutenants to put in command of the small groups of men he scattered around the countryside to gather in the cattle, and this meeting would give him a chance to form some opinion of which men to select.

Greg Haslett looked like a good man to make one of the straw bosses. That feller Washman had the look of a top hand and would make another. An obvious third would be John Poe, but Dusty had to avoid showing any favor towards the JA as his uncle owned it.

"This here's Saul Bunyon," Chisum said.

"Rode in the 3rd New Mexican Volunteers in the War," Sanders put in.

Dusty glanced at Sanders, then saw anger creep into Bunyon's eyes. The War might be over, but its old scars remained and nothing could blow up trouble like mentions of who wore which color uniform. Nor was Dusty fooled by Sanders' remark. As one of the South's better know cavalry leaders, Dusty might be expected to show less favor to a man who rode on the Union side.

Knowing the problem, Dusty nipped it in the bud, before it could flower.

"That so, Saul?" he said. "They were a good outfit. I'm pleased I never had to tangle with them, they might not have been so easy to handle as some of the eastern regiments."

A grin of pleasure creased Bunyon's face. Like most old soldiers, he had a soft spot in his heart for his regiment. Hearing the 3rd New Mexican Volunteers praised in such a manner by Dusty Fog chilled down his resentment towards Sanders.

The thing which annoyed Dusty about the whole affair was that neither Bunyon nor his foreman struck the small Texan as being straw-boss material. Only he would have to take one of them now to dispel any thought that he might be dwelling on Civil War loyalties should he not take them.

"War's long over," Dusty went on, looking around him. "We're running a roundup, not starting it again."

A rumble of agreement came from the other men, even Sanders joining in. It seemed that Dusty had made his point.

There was much more needing to be settled, a host of details that all the men wished to discuss. Dusty glanced at the wall clock and saw that Candy was taking her full twenty minutes.

"It's pay night," he said. "Let's leave business until tomorrow. We'll meet in the backroom, if Candy will let us, and get down to arrangements at noon tomorrow, if that suits you all?"

"I'm for it," Chisum grunted, having hovered in the background.

"Sure," Bunyon went on. "Let's have us a whing-ding tonight. Something tells me we're going to be worked for the next few weeks."

"One thing I can promise all of you for sure," Dusty

drawled. "You will be, I'll see to that."

"How about joining us for a drink, Cap'n Fog?" Sanders asked.

At that moment Dusty saw Candy coming down the stairs. Only it was not the same girl who went up. No longer did she wear the skin-tight, revealing gown or the makeup on her face and had even left off most of her jewelry. Her hair had been taken up into a pile on top of her head and a small, not too showy hat perched on it. The dress she wore was well-cut, modest in line, the kind of thing a rich rancher's wife, or an Army field rank officer's lady might wear.

"I'll take the drink later, gentlemen," he said. "Right now I have to take a lady out to supper."

CHAPTER FOUR

Mr. Chisum Consults His Attorney

Watching Dusty Fog escort Candy Carde from the saloon, Goodnight gave a contented sigh. He had studied the crowd's reactions as his nephew dealt with the three Long Rail men and knew that Dusty now had the cowhands solidly behind him. Most of the ranchers seemed to think that they had the best men handling their affairs and were content to accept Dusty's leadership. After watching Dusty impress the ranchers and foremen with his personality, Goodnight felt that he could now safely attend the conference in Houston knowing that the roundup was being handled to everybody's benefit and satisfaction.

Goodnight's view was not entirely shared by Chisum. While the Cattle King did not doubt that the roundup would be efficiently run, he knew his plans for making a vast profit out of it would be curtailed. He would be treated fairly, of that he was sure, but would get no more than was his due.

Swinging away from the excitedly talking ranchers and foremen, Chisum left the saloon. He scowled for a moment in the direction of Dusty and the girl, then turned and walked the opposite way, crossing Main

Street and making for a wooden building between the undertaker's shop and the billiard hall. A chink of light glinting by the edge of the curtain at the left side window told Chisum the man he wanted was at home. Chisum glanced up at a shingle which hung over the door.

"Hugo K. Scales," he read, "Attorney at Law."

A sniff which might have meant anything followed the words. Chisum knocked on the door, looking around to make sure that nobody was watching him. The few people on Main Street all seemed fully occupied with their own affairs and none paid any attention to the Cattle King. With his suspicious nature, Chisum did not want anybody to know he had business dealings with the lawyer. He stood outside the door for almost five minutes, scowling and muttering under his breath at the delay.

At last the door opened and Scales allowed the Cattle King to enter the building. Scales was tall, slim, handsome in a pink-and-white kind of way, and always dressed well. However, at the moment his hair was untidy; he did not wear a jacket and his vest was unfastened while his shirt showed signs of being hurriedly adjusted for one of the buttons tucked through the wrong hole.

"You got company?" asked Chisum, sniffing the air of the hall in which he stood.

"A client just left," Scales answered, sounding as if he expected the subject to be closed with his words.

"Did, huh?"

Nobody had left the building by its front entrance since Chisum knocked. The hall in which he stood led to a rear door through which a client might slip unseen. Especially a client who wore perfume and who had been in the left side room, which definitely was not Scales' office. Chisum knew Scales to be something of a dandy dresser and as such would be highly unlikely to interview a lady on *legal* business while attired in such an untidy manner.

A scowl creased Scales' brow as he opened the door of his office and waved Chisum inside. The Cattle King stood sniffing like a redbone hound seeking coon scent. There was no trace of the perfume he had smelled in the hall, which did not entirely surprise the Cattle King.

The sniffs drew an even deeper frown from Scales. Back East he had been fed on a diet of professional respect and it galled him to have an uncouth Westerner, who boasted that he could barely read or write, treat him in such a manner. However, Scales kept his thoughts to himself. He owed a lot to Chisum for the normal legal business in Goodnight would never have kept him in a manner to which he felt his tastes should become accustomed. The Cattle King paid well for certain not entirely legal services Scales rendered.

Part of Scales' duties, in addition to acting as the Cattle King's go-between and voice, were to help Chisum plot ways and means which would bring the rancher whatever he wanted. Scales had thought up a smart plan to ensure that Chisum's representative became roundup captain, and the lawyer wondered how his scheme worked out.

"How did it go at the saloon?" Scales asked.

"Bust. That lousy, woman-chasing Bonney came too late and another man beat him to it."

"Get rid of—"

"If it was that easy, I'd've done it by now!" Chisum barked. "You tell me where I can get a man who'll stack up against Dusty Fog, and I'll hire him."

"How about Jesse Evans?"

"Jesse's no fool. Bonney wouldn't stack up against Dusty Fog, neither will Jesse."

"But what went wrong?" asked Scales, then his handsome face twisted into a scowl. "Do you think she double-crossed us—No, she wouldn't dare, with what I have on her."

"It was a mistake. We can't blame her for it."

"I told her to watch for a group of men riding in. One of them wearing dark clothes and riding a white horse, which is how Bonney dressed and rode—"

"And the Ysabel Kid dressed in all black, rides a damned great white stallion," Chisum commented bitterly. "She made a mistake."

"That's what it was. It must have been. Vi—Candy wouldn't dare go against me. She did the rest all right?"

"Sure, came over, tried to goose us along to make the decision. Bit on what I said about her picking the man and fed us the idea of taking the first one through the door. If Bonney had come—"

"But he didn't!" Scales snarled.

The lawyer felt angry at the failure of his plan. It had been well made and he had never expected it to go wrong. Perhaps there might have been difficulty in persuading the ranchers to go for the first-through-the-door idea, but Scales guessed correctly, that most of the men would go for anything Chisum appeared to be against. Everything had gone off smoothly— except for the most important detail of all.

"You got any more ideas?" Chisum asked.

"You can't get this Dusty Fog removed?"

"Man, you know the West, do you?" Chisum snorted. "Dusty Fog's the man who ran the Rocking H trail herd into Dodge City when Wyatt Earp put the Injun sign on the outfit and said it hadn't got to come."*

"Surely you've enough men—"

Quickly Chisum told Scales of his three hands' abortive attempt to deal with the Rio Hondo gun wizard. He explained in profane detail how the three men tried to get an edge by fighting with their bare hands, and were soundly whipped for their pains. Scales' frown deepened when he heard of Candy Carde's ac-

*Told in *Trail Boss*.

tions and that the girl had gone to supper with Dusty Fog. Then the lawyer shrugged his shoulders. The friendship might be turned to his advantage and he hinted as much to the Cattle King.

"You try and he'll drop her like she was red hot," Chisum growled. "He's not one of your cowhands, ready to flop on his back and kick his legs in the air because a pretty gal smiles at him."

"Let me think about it then," Scales replied.

"Think hard. I aimed to drive out Haslett, Dickens and Naylor with his roundup, and I don't like being disappointed."

"Well, I talked with all three men a few days ago. None of them want to sell out."

"Did you let 'em know who's behind the offer?"

One of the many things which annoyed Scales in his dealings with Chisum was the way the Cattle King appeared to expect him to make the most foolish and elementary mistake.

"I said some eastern syndicate was buying," Scales explained. "And I've a forged letter to prove it. I thought we might get Naylor's place. But he insists on staying on."

"If I'd got Bonney in as roundup captain, I'd've had Naylor, Dickens and Haslett begging me to buy 'em out."

"We still might do something, Mr. Chisum. Let me think on it."

"You sure you've got that Carde gal under control and on a tight rein?" Chisum asked. "She won't tell Dusty Fog about today?"

"Not as long as I know what I know."

"And what's that?"

A superior smile came to Scales' lips. "A lawyer never betrays his clients' confidences."

"The hell you don't," Chisum scoffed. "So play cagey, but don't blame me when she slips through your fingers."

Neither man spoke for a time. A thought came to Scales, one which scared him far more than he wanted to admit even to himself. Suppose the girl folks in Goodnight knew Candy Carde had grown tired of living in his power. She might have taken up with a man who not even Billy Bonney would face so as to be free of Scales' domination. That did not seem likely. While Dusty Fog might be able to hold off Cornwall's men he would not protect the girl from the law.

Another train of thought came to Scales, springboarded by the memory of something Chisum had said earlier about Candy Carde going to supper with Dusty Fog. For all his faults, Scales was a shrewd judge of human nature, and knew how people in these small frontier towns thought and acted. Handled correctly, the friendship with Candy Carde might blast Dusty Fog from his position.

"How good a man is Fog with cattle?" he asked.

"Damned good. Charlie Goodnight helped teach him and Charlie allows he's one of the best for his age in Texas."

"I see. Suppose you were roundup captain and doing it for everybody's benefit, not just your own, where would you start the men working?"

"Down here on the southern ranges around town, then work my way north."

"Then Dusty Fog's likely to do it that way too?"

"I'd reckon so," Chisum replied. "Why?"

Scales did not reply for a moment. Whatever else he might think about Chisum, the lawyer acknowledged that the rancher was a master at the cattle business. So if Chisum would have started his roundup down by the town, it seemed more than likely that Dusty Fog would do the same. If so, Scales had the nucleus of an idea. Despite what Chisum said, Scales believed he still had a strong enough hold on Candy to make her behave and carry out his orders.

"It's just an idea. Leave things until Monday and

I'll tell you all about it, Mr. Chisum."

Not knowing he was being plotted against, Dusty Fog entered the Bauman Café with Candy Carde on his arm. Their entrance attracted some attention, for there was a fair crowd in the room. A group of soberly dressed, generally sour-featured women seated at a table on the right of the room all stopped eating and talking to stare towards the door.

"That's the Good Ladies of Goodnight League," Candy remarked. "We have a mutual disagreement pact. I don't like them and they loathe me."

"They ever met you?" Dusty answered.

"Only to step off the sidewalk as I pass. I'm a scarlet woman, or didn't you know?"

Dusty smiled at the girl and gently squeezed her arm. "I didn't, but it might be fun finding out."

One of the women stared hard at Dusty, then started to tell the others something. From the way they reacted, her news came as something of a surprise to her friends. It caused some tongue-clucking and head-shaking.

"Let's go, Dusty," Candy said quietly. "I shouldn't have come with you in the first place. Those old hens know who you are, and they're not going to like their roundup captain being out at supper with me."

"Then they're going to have to lump it," drawled Dusty. "Let's go. That table out in the center looks just about right to me."

For a moment Candy hung back. She suddenly realized the position her friendship might put Dusty in. Although she needed the kind of help only a man such as Dusty Fog could give her, Candy had no desire to ruin him, or cause him any extra trouble. From what she had learned about cattle work, Candy knew that a roundup captain had quite enough on his hands without adding the enmity of the good ladies of the town to his troubles.

"It's no go—" she began.

"We'll make less of a scene if you walk over than if I pick you up and carry you," Dusty replied. "Come on, girl. If you've done anything to be ashamed of in town, walk out. If not you're eating supper with me."

The words steadied Candy. Certainly she had never given the women of the town any cause for their behavior. She ran a straight, clean saloon and her girls entertained only in the barroom. Throwing a look of gratitude mingled with something more at Dusty, Candy allowed him to escort her to the central table. He drew out a chair for her, seated her, then took the chair at her right hand.

"Dustine," Candy breathed. "I'll never forget this."

"You'll be making me blush next," he smiled.

At that moment Mark, the Kid and Waco entered. The three men stood at the door, looked around the room and started to walk across it towards a side table. Candy nodded to them and asked Dusty to call them over.

"We may as well," she smiled. "It will give the Good Ladies something to really get their teeth into."

"Or make them think this is all innocent," Dusty answered.

"Do it, Dustine," she breathed. "For me."

"For me, you mean," Dusty said. "All right, but it sure makes me wonder."

Much to their surprise, Mark and the other two saw Dusty signal them to join him. Mark caught on first, nodding his head to where the Good Ladies sat in their vicious little circle.

"Danged old hens," he breathed. "Let's go join Candy and Dusty."

The meal was pleasant, with good food, coffee and light-hearted conversation to make it better. Candy laughed, but never raucously or in an unlady-like manner, talked in her quiet, well-modulated voice and clearly enjoyed herself. Through all the meal she gave no hint of where she worked; and did nothing to de-

serve the looks and head-shakes directed in her direction by the Good Ladies of Goodnight League.
From the way she acted, a stranger would have taken
Candy as the well brought-up sister of one of the
quartet enjoying a meal with her brothers and his
friends.

Shortly before the meal ended, Dusty saw Naylor
and a woman enter the café. The slim young rancher
looked towards where Dusty's party were seated.

"Captain Fog," he said as the four Texans rose to
their feet. "I'd like you to meet my wife. Laura, this
is Miss Carde—"

"Charmed," purred Laura Naylor, throwing a surprised glance at Candy as if she could not believe the
notorious saloonkeeper dressed in such a manner.

"Enchanted," Candy answered.

Sparks struck from the first words. Laura Naylor
stood a couple of inches taller than Candy, had brunette hair taken up on top of her head, a beautiful
face—yet one which had a touch of hardness and
imperious snobbery about it—and a figure that the
dark green dress emphasized as being well worth looking at. Two things were obvious to the men: first,
Laura did not like Candy; second, that the dislike was
mutual.

"Captain Fog, I told you of him on the way here,
dear," Naylor went on, trying to cover up his for
wife's behavior. "Mark Counter, the Ysabel Kid and
Waco."

"Good evening," she said coolly. "Sit down,
please."

"May we join you Captain?" Naylor asked.

"Feel free," Dusty replied.

Naylor and his wife sat at the table and a waitress
appeared to take their order. For a moment none of
the party spoke, then Naylor gave a nervous grin and
looked at Dusty.

"I'm afraid I won't be much use to you on the

roundup, Captain," he said. "Do we need all this formality? I'm Jim and my wife is Laura to our friends."

"Make it Candy, Dusty, Mark, Lon and Waco then," Dusty replied. "And don't you worry none, we'll find something for you to do."

"Yes, sir, that's for sure," drawled the Kid. "A roundup captain's a feller's don't need sleep, and sure makes certain nobody else gets any."

"Dusty's a mite that ways all the time," Waco went on.

Turning her eyes to Dusty, Laura Naylor asked, "Have you had considerable experience in such matters as this, Dusty?"

"Comes to a push I can just about tell a bull from a cow," Dusty replied. "I take turns with a couple of my cousins back to home with our roundups."

"Then you could tell from the result of a roundup whether a ranch is likely to succeed or not?"

"Your ranch?"

"Any ranch."

Dusty glanced at Naylor, then at Laura before answering her question.

"You've only been on the range for nine months," he pointed out.

"But surely one could form an idea—"

"We shouldn't be bothering Dusty with things like that, dear," Naylor put in, clearly embarrassed by the line his wife's questions took.

"But one has to ask somebody," Laura answered. "After all, dear, you can hardly set yourself up as an authority on ranching."

"I suppose not, dear. But let's leave it, shall we?'

"Just as you say," Laura purred. "By he way, Dusty, we're giving an informal dinner party tomorrow evening. I hope you will come."

While not being anti-social, Dusty had no wish to attend the dinner. He did not wish to be put in the position of having accepted one rancher's invitation when he would not have time to accept others. All too well Dusty knew the tricky nature of his work, that he must keep a careful balance between the various ranch crews. More than anything, Dusty wanted to avoid giving anybody a chance to hint at favouritism.

"Candy, the boys and I are guests at Colonel Goodnight's place tomorrow," he said, knowing he could rely on his uncle to cover up for him by extending an invitation.

"But I sent an invitation to the Colonel only this evening," Laura answered. "I insist that you all come out to our place. I'm having the rest of the ranchers and their families, as well as some of the civic dignitaries along. It will give you a chance to meet them. I expect you, too, Miss Carde, unless your business won't permit it."

"I've never opened my place on Sundays," Candy answered, sounding like a bobcat meeting another on a log.

"Then you'll be free to come," Laura purred back. "Now, can I expect you all, Dusty?"

Ignoring Candy's gentle kick across the leg, Dusty nodded his agreement. If he arrived at the dinner, he would damned soon be able to make it clear that his judgment as roundup captain would not be affected by the invitation.

"We'll be there, ma'am."

"At eight sharp," she replied. "I've seen the Reverend Veasey and it will allow the guests time to come out to our place after church."

Soon after Dusty's party left the Naylors. Outside the café Candy stopped and looked at Dusty.

"I can't go tomorrow," she said.

"Why not?" Dusty replied. "Damn it, Candy, up in Kansas a girl who runs a saloon's mayor of Mulrooney, a town that is four times the size of Goodnight. She's welcome in the best houses, so I'm damned sure you are down here. Now either you go tomorrow, or I don't."

"But if you don't," Candy objected, "They'll think that—"

"Why sure. So you've got to go to keep up your good name."

Mark and the other two cowhands had walked on along the street, heading for the Juno Saloon. Looking at Dusty, Candy smiled, a gentle smile which lit up her eyes. No man had ever treated her as did this soft-spoken Texan.

"You're building trouble for yourself, Dustine," she warned.

"So you keep telling me," he replied. "Come on, let's go back to the Juno and see if we can't build up some more."

CHAPTER FIVE

My Client Won't Like This, Miss Carde

In accordance with Dusty's suggestion, the roundup's organization meeting was held at noon the following day. All the ranchers and their foremen were gathered in the spacious back room of the Juno Saloon when Dusty and Mark entered shortly after twelve o'clock. None of the men raised any objections to the two Texans being a few minutes late, for Goodnight had told the others what kept his nephew away. Dusty and his three *amigos* rose at dawn, took their horses from the stable of Goodnight's town house and spent several hours checking the local range. Now, while the Kid and Waco tended to the quartet's horses, Dusty and Mark joined the rancher owners to settle the business of running the roundup.

First each rancher told Dusty how many of his men he would be sending on the main roundup. The JA, Flying M, and the Long Rail, as the biggest ranches in the area would each send a chuckwagon. Every ranch brought along its own remuda of spare horses for its hands. All the expenses of the roundup would be shared among the ranchers in proportion to the number of cattle they owned and the acreage of land under each brand's control.

Up to that point all went smoothly and without question, for it had become standard range procedure. Nor did any of the ranchers, even Chisum, object when Dusty stated that they would work the southern ranges first and move north. All present who knew the cattle business would have made the same decision had they been in Dusty's position.

"How about the dough-nuts and mavericks, Cap'n?" Sanders asked, bringing up the most controversial issue of the entire roundup.

By tradition a calf belonged to whatever ranch owned its mother. However many a calf grew up and separated from its mother without feeling the touch of a branding iron, or without having a mark of ownership placed on it while it was still at its mother's side, so that no definite proof of ownership could be established. Such unbranded animals were assumed to belong to the first man to slap a brand on their hides and were termed mavericks. Dough-guts were calves that had lost their mothers early and reared themselves on a diet of grass and water. Such food tended to be too heavy for the young stomachs to handle properly and in time the belly swelled like a mix of sourdough in a burlap sack. While the dough-guts looked weak creatures, they would fatten up and grow into saleable beef. Having lost their mothers, the dough-guts could not be claimed by any ranch and so were classed as mavericks.

"This range's swarming with strays and mavericks, Cap'n," Haslett remarked before Dusty could give a decision for or against the unbranded stock problem.

"So the Kid told me," Dusty replied.

While the Comanches rarely ate beef, they often raided cattle drives which passed through their country. The attacks, even if not successful in halting the march of the white man's progress, caused either stampedes or just a running of the herd and the loss of some of its stock. Some of the cattle so left behind had been gathered by the Comanches to sell either to Mexicans or Comanchero traders. The Comanches had never possessed the knowledge, skill or desire to make a thorough roundup and as a result hundreds of cattle from southern ranches roamed the range living and breeding. While the original strays bore brands, and so did not class as mavericks, their offspring had never been branded and did.

On Dusty's solution to the maverick problem might depend the success of the roundup. If he made the wrong decision it could lead to bad feeling among the various ranches involved.

"I reckon we'll pool all the unbranded stuff," Dusty suggested, "then share it out among you in proportion to the size of your spread."

A low rumble went up among the men. Ranchers and their foremen exchanged words in low tones and Dusty made no attempt to interrupt. He and Mark sat at the table and waited until the talk ended.

"Allus reckoned the outfit who gathered the maverick claimed it," Chisum said. Knowing the situation, he had intended to make sure that the majority of the unbranded stock came his way. "That's the way it's done on most roundups."

"So they tell me," Dusty answered dryly. "Only this isn't like most other roundups, Mr. Chisum. All of you moved into what amounts to new country less than a year ago. Your stock's all been on the range about the same time and any unbranded grown stuff you brought in is your own fault. There's not been a bad enough winter for many cows to have died off and left dough-guts. So if you all take a share of the mavericks, it'll be fair to you all."

"That sounds reasonable enough to me," Bunyon stated and Sanders gave a low growl of agreement.

"I've seen this idea of 'the one who gathers the maverick claims it' at work," Goodnight put in. "You get the hands looking for unbranded stock and leaving the branded stuff behind. Or some smart gent starts making dough-guts with a rifle, which same starts trouble."

"Let's put it to the vote," Dusty said. "All in favor show your right hands, gents."

Only the ranchers voted on the matter, although Naylor looked at his foreman who gave a nod of agreement. Nine hands rose into the air and, after a momentary hesitation, Chisum made the decision unanimous. Not that Chisum failed to see how Dusty had reached the fairest solution to the problem. Chisum had never meant to play fair with the others. If his plan to have Bonney put in as roundup captain had worked, and with Goodnight out of the way, Chisum planned to hog the majority of the unbranded stock for himself. With Dusty in command there would be no chance of Chisum's plan succeeding. So he decided that as long as he could not have his own way, Long Rail might as well take its fair share with the others.

With the matter of the mavericks settled to everyone's satisfaction, Dusty went on to tell the other men what he wanted and how he intended to work the roundup. He arranged their first gathering point, told the ranchers that Mark would be his segundo and detailed off the straw bosses he would need.

"I want a tally man," he finished and looked around the table.

"How about me, Dusty?" Naylor asked as nobody else offered to volunteer. "I'm not much use as a cowhand, but Greg's told me the tally man's duties and I reckon I can handle them."

Nobody raised any objections. The tally man had a responsible task and one demanding scrupulous honesty. However, it was not gruellingly hard work and mostly went to a man, provided he had the necessary clerical ability, who was unable to cope with more strenuous duties. Naylor was not a strong man due to ill-health; but he possessed the necessary qualifications to handle the tally book, recording the number of calves and unbranded animals belonging to each spread as they were branded by the hands.

"That's about all then, gents," Dusty said. "Anybody got anything they want to bring up?" He waited for a time but none of the others spoke, so he went on, "We'll meet on that flat land tomorrow at sun up and start the first circles and gathers from there."

Chairs scraped back and men rose to their feet. Talking among themselves, the ranchers giving orders to their foremen, all left the backroom and crossed the empty barroom to the front doors. Naylor turned just before he left and looked at Dusty and Mark.

"Don't forget tonight. We'll be expecting you at about half-past seven."

"We'll be there," Dusty replied.

After the ranchers and foremen left, Dusty locked the front doors. He and Mark walked back across the barroom and up the stairs leading to the first floor.

"That went off easy enough," Mark drawled. "I thought Chisum would have made more trouble."

"He may try it yet. When Chisum gives in too easy I get suspicious and start looking for the joker in the deck. Come on, Mark, Candy'll be waiting lunch for us."

"Likely will. I hope she cooks as good as she looks, sings and dances."

"It wouldn't surprise me if she did," Dusty said. "She's a right smart lil gal."

"Looks good, too," grinned Mark.

"I hadn't given it a thought," Dusty replied, also grinning.

On their return from supper the previous evening, Candy changed back into her working clothes and took part in the saloon's small stage show. Not only did she prove to have a good singing voice and an ability to tell a joke, but she joined some of her girls in a high-kicking, leg-showing dance which went down real well with the audience.

After her appearance on the stage, Candy joined

Dusty's party at the table reserved for ranchers and other local dignitaries. Dusty had studied the girl as she took a seat at his side. She looked flushed, excited and delighted; and he guessed that she loved being out in front of a crowd, entertaining them and receiving their approval and applause. More than ever Dusty wondered why a gal like Candy would bury herself and her talents in a small town. With her love for entertaining, and her beautiful face and shapely body, she could have commanded prices in theaters anywhere that would make her earnings from the saloon like a pittance.

Dusty had asked no questions. Both he and Candy enjoyed a pleasant evening, arranged to lunch together the following day after the meeting and parted at her door.

Although the lunch proved to be excellent, Candy confessed she had not cooked it. With the meal over, Dusty and Candy took a buggy ride together. They left Mark, the Kid and Waco entertaining some of Candy's girls in a hilarious game of poker that had little or no connection with the scientific play credited to have been devised by Hoyle.

Neither Dusty nor Candy noticed the curtain of Lawyer Scales' living quarters' window lift as they passed. Scales stood at the window and watched the buggy as it went out of sight. Turning from the window, the lawyer paced his room. A scowl creased his brow as he thought of Candy and her new friend. While not being range-bred, Scales had heard enough of Dusty Fog to know the small Texan might easily jeopardize his hold on the girl. The lawyer decided to see Candy at the first opportunity and learn how things stood between her and Dusty Fog.

At four o'clock Dusty brought Candy back to town. They left the girl's buggy in the livery barn and Candy arranged with the owner to borrow one of his horses to take her out to the Naylor place that evening.

"I'll tend to it, Miss Candy," the man promised. "Got a bay in the corral that'll do you fine."

"Make sure it has some life in it, Joe," she replied. "I want to keep up with Captain Fog's horse."

"I'll promise you that bay can do it," grinned the old owner of the barn.

"I thought you'd rather ride your horse—on the way out," Candy remarked as she left the barn on Dusty's arm.

"Why sure. It'll be daylight," Dusty replied. "Coming back though—"

"Yes, Dustine?"

"Well, it won't be daylight then."

"I know. And I get so frightened in the dark."

"So do I," Dusty said and gently squeezed her arm. "We'd best ride back in the buggy."

"When I'm frightened I like to creep up close to somebody," Candy warned.

"Now that's strange. When I'm scared, I like somebody to creep up real close to me. Let's hope it's a good dark night."

"Shucks," Candy replied. "When I'm with the right—Anyway, I get scared even when it's not too dark."

They had reached the front of the saloon by that time and separated at the door. Watching Dusty walk away, Candy gave a sigh. If only she had met that soft-spoken, *big* man before—But she had not met him before. Now their paths had crossed, Candy did not want anything to come between her and Dusty.

In her rooms Candy found her arrangements had been attended to. She had three rooms, a small sitting and dining room, a bedroom and a small bathroom. In the latter a bath full of hot water waited her. Stripping off her clothes, Candy put up her hair and climbed into the bath, laying back in the water and thinking of Dusty Fog.

Candy had just finished her bath and was drying

herself when one of her girls knocked on the bathroom door and said Mr. Scales was waiting to see her. A cold, sinking feeling hit Candy. Yet she knew she could not refuse to see the man.

"Tell him I'll be out in a few minutes," she said.

Ten minutes later Candy walked into the sitting room and found Scales lounging in a chair. The girl wore a robe over her underclothing and had slippers on her feet. She looked at the elegant lawyer for a moment and asked:

"What do you want?"

"I just received a message from your—friend."

"And?"

"He wants something doing," Scales told the girl, noting the anxiety in her voice.

"Such as?"

"Such as getting Dusty Fog to run the roundup his way."

"That's out!"

The words cracked like a pop of a bull-whacker's whip from Candy's lips. She stood glaring defiantly at the man who brought messages from the mysterious person who ruled her life.

"You won't do it?"

"No!"

"Suppose he was to inform—"

"Suppose I was to tell Dustine of the whole business?" she countered.

"It wouldn't be wise, Miss Carde," Scales answered. "My—client wouldn't hesitate to inform the Pinkertons of your presence here in Goodnight."

"I don't think Dustine would be frightened by the Pinkertons."

"Possibly not—if the Pinkertons came alone. But they would have extradition papers to take you back, and the Texas Rangers would have to honor the order. Captain Fog might be infatuated with—"

Stepping forward, Candy brought her right hand

lashing around in a slap which landed hard enough to jerk Scales' head over to one side and almost knocked the lawyer from his chair. Sacles threw the chair over backwards and came to his feet. Never had Candy seen such a concentration of rage and fury on a man's face. She took a hurried step to the rear, her fingers crooked ready to defend herself.

It may have been common sense, or the sight of Candy standing bristling like an alley-cat and ready to defend herself, that caused Scales to exert his self-control and stopped him in his tracks. For a moment he stood rubbing a hand on his cheek; the girl's fingers had left their mark. Then slowly he turned and set the chair on its legs once more.

"I asked for the slap, Miss Carde," he said, the words coming out cold and angry. "But my client won't like this, Miss Carde. Captain Fog might stand against the Pinkertons, but he won't face the Rangers; not because he is afraid of them, but because they will tell him why they were taking you in to be returned to New Orleans."

In her heart Candy knew the lawyer spoke the truth. She had learned much about Dusty Fog in the short time they knew each other. Possibly Dusty might protect her, but could she ask him to throw aside everything and become a wanted outlaw for her sake? Candy did not doubt that he would do so. Yet she knew she could never ask him to make the sacrifice.

"I won't try to use my influence, if I have any, on Dustine," she told Scales. "Nor will I put him in the position of having to refuse me. Dustine is a gentleman, Mr. Scales. He gave his word to bring this roundup off successfully, and he wouldn't break it for me."

"Possibly not."

"Definitely not. Who is this client, I've never seen him."

"Nor will you. He works through me—"

"Dustine might be able to find him."

"And learn how you're using him?"

Candy sucked in a deep breath. Then she pointed to the door leading to the passage.

"Get out!" she snapped. "And tell your client that if anything goes wrong with this roundup I'll tell Dustine everything."

"My client won't like that, Miss Carde," Scales replied. "He's a bitter and vindictive man. If I was you, Miss Carde, I'd walk warily and think twice before crossing him."

Watching Scales leave her rooms, Candy felt sick and frightened. She gave thought to flight, slipping out of town and disappearing into the west. Common sense told her such an idea was foolish. There was no stage out of town and a woman traveling alone in any other type of conveyance would attract too much attention. She decided that on the way back from Naylor's party she would tell Dusty everything and then get in touch with the Rangers to let them arrange her return to New Orleans.

On his way from the saloon, Scales decided that his client would want Candy taught a lesson, given a sharp warning of who was boss. While walking back to his home, Scales thought of something he had heard the previous evening. He quickened his pace and by the time he reached the building which bore his shingle he had the plan thought out. Only a few small details needed fixing and Miss Candy Carde as she called herself would learn it did not pay to cross Lawyer Scales' client.

Candy's buggy, with the livery barn horse harnessed to it, stood before the Juno Saloon. The livery barn's owner had brought the rig across a few minutes early so that he could enjoy a quick, free snifter of Candy's whisky before returning to his place of business.

None of the four cowhands gave more than a casual glance at the tall man in cowhand style clothing who

walked away from the rig as they came into sight
further along the street. Dusty, Mark and the Kid were
too engrossed in coping with Waco's arguments against
his going with them to the Naylor place to pay any
attention to the man as he had left the side of the
buggy's horse. He passed out of sight down the alley
between the saloon and the general store next door,
and by the time Dusty's party reached the end of the
alley had gone from sight.

"Can't see why I need go," Waco objected, not
for the first time. "Anyways there's that lil gal—"

"Sure," Dusty replied, his seventeen-hand paint
stallion ranging alongside the youngster's mount which
was just as big and also a paint. "There's the lil gal
that you're wanting to improve. Only you're coming
with us."

"Sure are," agreed Mark Counter, leveling his huge
bloodbay stallion on the other side of Waco's uncut
stud horse.

"You're coming and you'll like it," the Kid stated
firmly, his great white stallion cutting off Waco's
retreat from the rear. That horse looked two shades
meaner and a whole heap wilder than a starving silver-
tip grizzly bear just out of its winter den-hole.

"So I'll come," Waco growled. "Only I won't like
it."

They halted their horses before the saloon. Tossing
his paint's reins to Waco, Dusty swung from his saddle, crossed the sidewalk and went to the door of the
saloon. It opened and Candy came out. From all signs
Candy had taken especial care of her appearance. Her
hair was taken up and she wore a stylish hat. The
cloak she wore covered her dress, but it rustled in the
manner only silk could.

Taking the girl's arm, Dusty escorted her to the
buggy and helped her into the driving seat.

"Reckon you can handle things," he asked with a
grin.

"I reckon I can," she replied, unfastening the reins.

Swinging on his heels, Dusty walked back to his horse. The bay harnessed to the buggy was a fine looking animal, one with a heap of spirit. It moved gently in the harness showing eagerness to get moving. Feeling the reins touch its body as Candy raised them, the horse thrust itself forward into the harness straps. Instantly a change came to it. With a scream of pain, the bay reared on its hind legs and then flung itself forward. Candy was slammed back into the seat. Luckily she managed to stay in the buggy, but she lost her hold of the reins.

The buggy, dragged wildly behind the bay, rocketed off down Main Street. Candy clung to her seat, hanging on and unable to reach the trailing reins. Of the four Texans, Dusty reacted first. He took one look at the runaway bay, then ran forward to go afork his seventeen-hand stallion in a single bound and without touching the stirrup irons until he hit the saddle. On landing in the saddle, Dusty jerked the reins from Waco's hands and at the same moment applied his Kelly petmaker spurs to the paint's flanks. An instant after Dusty's paint started running, his three *amigos* sent their mounts on its heel. All rode as they had never ridden before, for they saw the danger to Candy Carde.

Hooves thundered in Main Street. People leaving the little church stopped to stare. Recognizing the girl in the buggy, some of the women were inclined to cluck their tongues and leap to the conclusion that Candy was taking part in a cowhand prank.

Only when the careering buggy came closer did the people realize that they were witnessing something more serious than cowhand high-spirits. The sight of the racing vehicle and the four big horses tearing after it sent people scattering out of the way.

Dusty brought the big paint along the right side of the buggy. Twisting in his saddle, he saw the frightened face of the girl turn towards him. He read fear but not panic on the girl's face.

"Move this way, Candy!" he yelled.

Already the Kid was passing Dusty at the right and Waco's paint inched forward by the left side. Ahead the street made a sharp turn and in its wild-eyed panic the bay would never manage to make a swing around it. Candy moved herself to the right side of the buggy and Dusty brought his paint closer in.

Looping the reins around his saddlehorn, Dusty gripped the girl around the waist, feeling her arms lock around his neck. Then he swung Candy from the buggy and kneed the paint away from the vehicle.

Waco and the Kid closed in on the bay, each leaning down to grab at the trailing rein. Showing their superb riding skill, each man grabbed hold of leather and then started to slow down their horses. Kicking his leg over the saddlehorn, Waco dropped to the ground, his high-heeled boots digging in as he tried to bring the panic stricken animal to a halt. The Kid left his white on the jump and lent the young blond a hand to control the struggling animal. Skilled horsemen that they were, it took Mark's assistance before the Texans managed to steady the sweating, wild-eyed bay.

Bringing his horse to the sidewalk edge, Dusty lowered the girl to her feet on it. Candy staggered slightly and Dusty leapt from his horse to give her his support. Behind them men and women hurried forward, the latter forgetting what Candy did for a living in their eagerness to learn what caused the horse to bolt.

The same thought had been in Mark, the Kid and Waco's minds. Leaving the other two to control the horse, Waco examined the harness. A low whistle left his lips as he looked at the back-band which attached the saddle-pad to the crupper.

"Lon, Mark," he said. "Just take a look here!"

Leaving Mark to control the horse, the Kid joined Waco.

"One thing's for sure," the Kid said as he looked at Waco's discovery. "This sure as hell wasn't no accident."

CHAPTER SIX

If She Goes, I Go With Her

Among the crowd which gathered was Ben Ewart, a lean, leathery old-timer who served as both county sheriff and town marshal. He looked ill at ease in his town suit and white shirt and tie, but having just left church stopped him wearing his gun. Drawing off his tie, Ewart opened his shirt neck and came forward. Ewart had a name for being a fair and good lawman, one Dusty and his three *amigos* would give their co-operation to.

"What happened, Miss Candy?" he asked, never for a moment thinking the girl had been indulging in a foolish joke.

"The horse just up and ran," she replied.

For a moment Ewart studied the horse. He knew the animal well, recognizing it as the pride of the livery barn; a spirited and fast animal, yet one not given to panic-stricken bolting.

"Up and ran?" he said. "I know that bay's a buggy-hauling fool, but I never once saw it just up and run."

An angry frown creased Dusty's brow as he looked at the lawman. Dusty had formed his opinion of Ewart—a favorable one to the marshal—and wondered if be might have made a mistake. However, before Dusty could speak, the Kid turned from where he and Waco stood examining the horse's harness and came forward.

"Tell you something, Ben," he said, holding out his hand. "Happen you'd had this stuck in your butt-end and you'd've run a mite too."

"This" proved to be a sharp thorned burr. The Kid let it rest on the palm of his hand so the others could see it. Taking his hand from Candy's arm, Dusty stepped forward and looked down.

"Where was it, Lon?" he asked, his voice low as the first gentle whisper of a Texas blue-norther storm.

"Under the back strap. Hoss wouldn't've felt a damned thing until it put weight to pulling. But when he started to pull—man, he'd feel like he backed butt first into a cactus."

"How in he—" Ewart began, then stopped himself, for it was Sunday and his wife objected to him using strong language on the Sabbath. "Just how did that burr get there?"

"That," Dusty answered, his voice still quiet, "is what I aim to find out. And *pronto*."

The Kid nodded to where the owner of the livery barn came along the street at a bow-legged gallop.

"Here's a man's might be able to tell us something, Dusty."

"Yeah," Dusty agreed. "He might at that."

"What happened?" asked the old man. "I heard Raider here bolted, but he's never done that afore."

"So I've heard." Dusty answered. "Did anybody go near the bay after you hitched it to the wagon?"

"Nope."

"No," Dusty drawled. "They couldn't have or the horse would have spooked when you led it out."

"Say, Dusty," Mark put in, coming from where he had stood holding the bay's head. "There was a feller standing by the horse as we turned on to Main Street.

Looked like a cowhand, I didn't give him more than a quick glance."

"Where'd he go?" asked Dusty, his voice that same quiet note but boding little good for the cowhand should they meet.

"Down the alley between the saloon and the place at this end."

"Go see what you can find, Lon."

"I'll take the boy with me, Dusty," replied the Kid. "Let's go, Waco."

Among other things, the Kid had been teaching Waco to read sign and found the youngster an apt pupil. Two pairs of eyes would be better than one on such a chore.

A low mutter went up from the crowd as they stood on the sidewalk or in the street and looked at the buggy. Ewart glanced at the crowd and his instincts as a lawman caused him to speak up.

"Come on, folks," he said, "it's all over now. Break it up and go home."

He might have found more difficulty in getting the crowd to go, but several of its members had been invited to the Naylors' party and wanted to make a start on the long journey to the ranch. Anyway, there did not appear to be any sign of further developments or excitement so they might as well go about their business. Another thing the crowd remembered was that Ben Ewart did not like to folk disobeying his orders and did not allow social standing to influence his decision when handling a law matter.

After the crowd had gone its separate ways, Ewart turned to look at Dusty as the small Texan stood at Candy's side.

"This wasn't any accident, Cap'n Fog," he said.

"It could have been a joke on somebody's part," Mark pointed out. "I've seen fellers put a burr under a hoss's saddle blanket for a joke."

"Who'd want to play a fool joke like that on Candy?"

Dusty asked, then a thought struck him. Turning to the barn's owner he went on, "Does anybody hire that bay regularly?"

"Not special, Cap'n. 'Course, ole Raider here's knowed as the fastest and best buggy hoss in the county."

"Did anybody ask about him today?"

"No, sir, Cap'n, only Miss Candy. She likes him when she's not using her own hoss."

Turning from the old man, Dusty looked at Candy and read the hint of trouble at the back of her eyes.

"Would anybody in town want to hurt you, Candy?"

Never had the girl thought so fast as after Dusty spoke. Candy had been expecting the question and already begun to think of an answer.

"The Good Ladies of Goodnight League don't like me. But I can't see them trying to get rid of me that way."

"Who else?" Dusty went on.

One word from Candy would see Dusty and his three *amigos* hunting up Lawyer Scales. Candy could guess that any of the quartet was fully capable of making the lawyer tell the identity of the mysterious man who controlled her life and gave her orders through Scales. Yet if they should try to do so, Scales would scream for the law. Candy knew enough about Bert Ewart to guess he would not allow the OD Connected men's reputations to prevent him from doing his duty. Either way the matter then went, Candy would lose friends. Besides, if Scales talked Dusty would learn Candy's secret. She wanted to be the one to tell him what drove her west, not for him to hear the news second hand.

"I can't think of anybody," she said. "I think it was just a stupid joke on somebody's part."

At that moment the Kid and Waco returned. Cowhand style, they had gone on their horses and rode swiftly back to the wagon. One look at their faces told Dusty that the Kid and Waco had nothing to report.

"That ground's too hard to show a track," the Kid drawled, swinging from his saddle.

"Feller couldn've gone anyplace once he went through the alley," Waco went on and a hopeful glint came to his face. "Say, I reckoned I ought to ask around, see if anybody saw the feller, then swing all round town looking for his tracks."

"That'd take some time, boy," Dusty pointed out. "We have to be at the Naylor place afore eight."

A grin came to Waco's lips, was replaced by a look of noble self-sacrifice and he replied, "I'll bear up under the blow."

"You'll bear up under my blow in a minute, boy," Mark warned. "If I've got to go to this shindig, so have you."

"For once I agree with Mark," Candy stated. "What now, Dustine?"

"We'll get you another horse for the buggy. You go tidy up and then we'll head for the Naylor place."

The delay caused Dusty's party to be the last of the guests to arrive at the Naylor place. Leaving Waco and the Kid to attend to the horses, Dusty and Mark escorted Candy to the well-lit front of the house. Just as they approached the front porch, the main door opened and Laura Naylor stepped out. She wore a stylish and expensive blue dress and some good jewelry glinted on her wrists and hands.

All in all the Naylor place showed signs of being backed by plenty of money. The house was larger than one might have expected for such a small spread and all the outbuildings were well-built.

"I'm so pleased to see you made it," Laura purred, coming forward. "I hear you nearly had an accident, Miss Carde."

"You might say that," Candy answered.

"I'm so pleased that you felt up to coming."

"I wouldn't have missed it for the world, after your gracious invitation, Mrs. Naylor," Candy replied.

"Come in, I'll show you where to put your cloak, Miss Carde. Captain Fog, Mr. Counter, you'll find the hat rack on the left of the door."

Laura Naylor stood aside to allow her guests to enter the house. The ground floor had a large room the front part of which was made into a sitting room; with a piano, small tables, a couple of sidepieces on which rested ornaments and vases, and several chairs. The rear of the area was the dining room, its long table already set and with the chairs around it ready for the guests. A wide flight of stairs rose up to the first floor and doors opened into the kitchen and other small downstairs rooms. In general the tone of the place, as with the building and the rest of the ranch, hinted at its owners being wealthy.

A hush fell over the room as Candy entered. Talk died down and every eye turned to the girl. Instantly the women in the room started clucking and got their heads together, although the men seemed to brighten up a trifle. All the cream of Goodnight's social elite were present, the ranchers, banker and his wife, Lawyer Scales and other local business men. Up until Candy entered there had been noise, chatter and laughter, now it died off.

"If this is Laura's idea of a joke—" one of the women said, loud enough for the words to reach Candy.

"The nerve, bringing that woman here!" another of the good ladies went on in a piercing whisper.

Red crept up over Candy's cheeks and her lips trembled. She had never felt so humiliated in her life. Every instinct told the girl to turn and dash from the room. Then Candy caught the mocking smile on Laura's face and realized that the other woman had invited her with the intention of humiliating her.

"Come along, Miss Carde," Laura said, her voice still the hateful purr. "Let me put your cloak away,

I'm sorry I haven't a maid."

"You've no need," Candy answered, trying to keep her voice even. "I'm not staying."

"Aren't you? That is a pity."

Just as Candy was about to turn, she felt Dusty's hand close on her arm. Candy glanced at the small Texan and was surprised at the cold, angry expression on his face.

"If she goes, I go with her," he said and he spoke loud enough for everybody in the room to hear him. His eyes, cold grey and angry, swept around the room and he went on, "Miss Carde came here at Mrs. Naylor's invitation, and with me as an escort. I take any slight to her as a personal insult."

Silence came down on the room once more. The ranchers and businessmen looked down at their wives and wondered what reaction the small Texan's words would bring. For their parts, the wives were struck dumb. They ruled the town of Goodnight and so far no man had dared cross them. Leaning against the side of the empty fireplace, Colonel Goodnight grinned broadly and shot out a hand to catch Naylor by the arm.

"Leave it be, Jim boy," the older man said with a grin. "It's time somebody handed that bunch their come-uppance and Dusty's just the boy to do it."

Dusty had a good memory for faces and it served him well at that moment. Stabbing out his hand, Dusty pointed at the banker and said, "Candy here's an owner of a business, the same as quite a few more of you. Take you, your bank has a good deposit of her money, doesn't it?"

"I can't discuss—"

"Think about one thing," Dusty interrupted. "She puts her takings into your bank, you get benefit of it. She's good enough for that." His eyes went went to the local freighter. "And you draw as much trade, if not more, from Candy than anybody in the area."

"Well!" the freighter's wife began and started to rise. "I've never—"

"Sit down, 'Melie!" growled the freighter. "You ain't going no place." He turned to Dusty. "I ain't gainsaying it, Cap'n. And I've never seen Miss Candy out of line on anything either in the saloon or out of it."

"Now you, marshal! You're a man who's handled a badge in more than one place and know the time of day. Did anybody ever come to you with a complaint of being robbed or mishandled in the Juno? Or have you ever had any trouble from the folks who work in it?"

"Nope, Cap'n Fog. It's a clean, straight house and I'm talking from experience. If every saloon was like it, the law'd have no complaints."

"Your wife helps you with women prisoners?"

"When there is any."

"We've never had any trouble from the Juno," the marshal's wife put in. "Miss Carde keeps her girls under control."

"And you, Mrs. Tappley," Dusty drawled, fixing the head of the Good Ladies of Goodnight League with his unwavering gave, "how much of your trade comes from Candy and her girls?"

"I—I—"

"It's Sunday, you've been to church?"

"This is an outrage—" Mrs. Tappley spluttered.

"Reckon your girls could get their clothes from some other place, Candy?"

A remarkable change came to Mrs. Tappley's face. All too well she knew how little trade her establishment would draw without the saloongirls' business. If Candy and her girls took their trade elsewhere, Mrs. Tappley would find it difficult to maintain her present standard of living.

"Miss Candy could start selling meals in the Juno," Mrs. Bauman remarked before Mrs. Tappley could reply. "It would go hard for me if she did."

"Up in Kansas there's a town four, five times as big as Goodnight," Dusty went on, "it's called Mulrooney and the mayor is a woman. Nobody holds it against her because she runs a saloon. Now you folks aren't going to sit here and tell me those Kansas crowd are more broad-minded than you."

Probably nothing could have changed the attitude of the Good Ladies than Dusty's last words. The women prided themselves on their up-to-date, tolerant and broad-minded attitudes. Now all of them exchanged glances, seeing the others were embarrassed by their behavior. Mrs. Tappley coughed, then rose and walked across the room.

"I—I'm thinking we owe you an apology, Miss Carde," she said. "I hope you will forget what happened and what was said on your arrival."

"It's forgotten," Candy replied.

A flicker of annoyance crossed Laura Naylor's face as she saw the way things had gone. She invited Candy in the hope of humiliating her and instead had brought social acceptance to the blonde. Worse, Laura now had somebody at her party who was as well-dressed, beautiful and shapely as herself. Like an evil queen of the fairy stories, Laura liked to be fairest of all in any company she found herself.

Once the ice had been broken, Candy set about consolidating her position and removing any remaining dislikes which the Good Ladies of Goodnight might feel towards her. She joined the other women, talking with them on their own terms and ignoring the men without any conscious effort. It soon became clear that Candy was at home in such company and inside five minutes had all the Good Ladies, with the exception of Laura Naylor, eating out of her hand. She showed the women just how wrong they had been about her and proved herself to be witty and intelligent instead of coarse and bawdy as they might have expected.

After watching for a time, Laura gave an annoyed

sniff and headed for the kitchen to return with word that dinner would shortly be served. Her guests gathered at the table, finding their places and sitting down. Some of the ladies showed, although they tried to hide it, concern at the sort of the formal lines of cutlery before them. A calculating glint came to Laura's eyes as she watched Candy sit down but failed to see any worry at having to select the right knife, fork or spoon.

The dinner, cooked and served by Mrs. Bauman's staff, went down well. By the time it had ended Candy was firmly established in the Good Ladies of Goodnight's good books; in fact, general mutters of agreement. Mrs. Tappley asked Candy to attend their next meeting with the view to being elected to membership of the League. Laura watched it all, trying to hide her frown and look as a hostess should.

During dinner Candy took time out to study Lawyer Scales' face. The young lawyer sat chatting amiably to Mrs. Tappley and when his eyes met Candy's, she could read nothing in them. If Scales did know about the attempt to either injure or frighten her, he showed no hint of the knowledge. Taking her cue from Dusty, Candy put off the scaring of her horse as a foolish prank when the matter was brought up by one of the other guests. She then changed the subject and started talking about the forthcoming roundup.

After dinner the party gathered in the front hall of the room once more. The women came together at the left of the room and the men merged at the right. Under such close conditions neither party could get down to enjoying themselves in complete freedom. Waco, who enjoyed this part of formal dinners when at home on the OD Connected, found things dull and looked around for some way to liven things up. His eyes came to rest on the piano, but he could not think how to get anybody to play it.

Laura Naylor caught the young Texan's eye and followed the direction of his gaze. An idea came to

her head, a chance to humiliate Candy Carde and also
for Laura to do something she wished to do. Rising
from her chair, she stepped into the center of the room.

"Quiet everybody, please," she said, waiting until
a hugh fell on the room. "I was wondering if Miss
Carde would entertain us."

The words met with a mixed reception. While the
ladies were now friendly with Candy, they did not
know if she could produce an entertainment suitable
for mixed ears. On the other hand, the men looked
forward to seeing and hearing some of Candy's entertainment but doubted if their wives would approve.

"That's an idea, ma'am," Waco put in. "Come on,
Miss Candy, let's hear a song."

For a moment Candy thought of refusing, then she
rose and walked across the room to the piano. It had
been two years or more since last she sat at such a
fine instrument and the temptation proved too much
for her to resist. Silk rustled and hissed as she took
her seat on the piano stool. Running her fingers along
the keys, Candy thrilled to hear the sound they made.
This was not a barroom instrument which had been
pounded by fingers in an attempt to compete with the
noise going on around it. Deftly she started to play a
haunting melody and began to sing. A complete hush
fell on the room as the music flowed out and annoyance creased Laura's face. Candy had once more risen
over a humiliation and come out of it with honors.

Applause came at the end of Candy's song and
requests for more rose on all sides. Candy smiled
around the room; the look Dusty had seen when she
sang and danced in the saloon came to her face once
more. Watching the girl, Dusty felt a touch of sadness.
Candy would never be happy without the applause
and approval of a crowd.

"Let's try a duet, Lon," Candy suggested, looking
at the Kid.

"Go on, Lon," Goodnight agreed.

After a little persuasion the Ysabel Kid joined Candy at the piano and they selected a song between them. Once more Candy's piano playing and singing held attention. The Kid was no mean hand at the singing game himself and gave the girl very able backing.

A hand fell on Dusty's arm when most of the guests were watching and listening to the duet. Turning, he found Laura Naylor at his side. The woman gave him a winning smile and whispered:

"Can I speak with you outside, Dustine?"

"Now?"

"It's important and I don't want to disturb the party, please come."

Dusty followed Laura from the room and on the porch she turned to face him.

"Will you do something for me, Dustine?"

"That depends on what it is."

"I—It's Jim, my husband. He's not a well man, Dustine, and should never have come out here. I'm afraid his being out on the ranch will kill him, for he is trying to do too much."

"How can I help?" Dusty asked, watching the woman's face and his nostrils picking up a trace of her perfume.

"After the roundup you could tell him the ranch is a failure, that it is so far gone that nothing could save it from bankruptcy. He would believe you, you are one of the men he admires."

"And suppose the ranch is sound?" Dusty countered. "From what I've seen of it so far, it might well be."

"You could still tell h—"

"I don't lie, Mrs. Naylor."

For a few seconds Laura stood studying Dusty's face. Failing to read anything from it, she turned and leaned her hands on the porch rail. She looked out across the dark rangeland and resentment glowed in her eyes, resentment mingled with fear. A chorus of coyote yips rang out around the place, blending in with the piano and singing from inside the house. A bull bellowed in the middle distance and beyond the sound came the distant haunting and spine-chilling scream of a cougar. Laura shuddered at the sound and swung to face Dusty.

"I hate this land," she said vehemently. "My nearest neighbor is twelve miles away. I'm cut off from everything that makes life worth living. Don't you see, Dustine. What woman of refinement would wish to stay out here?"

"My Cousin Betty manages well enough."

"But she's—" Laura began, then stopped as she remembered the note Dusty's voice held as he answered. He would not take kindly to any adverse comments about his cousin. "She was born to this life, Dustine. I wasn't. Will you help me get away?"

Although Dusty could guess at the loneliness of Laura's life, he also remembered something Goodnight had said the previous night. They had been talking about the various ranchers and Goodnight mentioned that Naylor came west for the sake of his health. Yet his wife wanted him to go back east again.

"I'll tell your husband the truth about whatever I find," he said. Inside the house, the singing stopped and applause welled up. "Maybe we'd better go in, Mrs. Naylor?"

"Go ahead. I'll follow you."

Laura stood and watched Dusty walk back into the house. Anger creased her face and she stamped her right foot on the porch's floor. It seemed that Dusty Fog was more than she bargained for. She had expected him to jump at the chance of helping her.

Just as Laura was about to enter the house, a voice spoke from the darkness at the end of the porch.

"I could have told you he wouldn't help, Laura."

Turning, she walked along the porch towards the dark shape. "Maybe you have a better idea?"

"Maybe I have. Let's go and talk about it."

"Not now. Somebody might miss us. I'll come into town tomorrow—No, you come out here, all our men will be away on the roundup."

"I'll be here sometime during the day."

Laura turned and went back to the house, standing at the door and watching her guests congratulating the singers. Nobody, not, even her husband, appeared to have missed her. She crossed the room and joined the others, starting to act like a perfect hostess again.

The rest of the party went off without incident and Mrs. Tappley insisted on Candy sharing her buggy on the way home. While Candy wanted to be alone with Dusty, she did not get a chance to refuse the offer. On the way back to town, Candy found herself helping to organize a show for the end of the roundup, the proceeds to go towards building a bigger and better church. However, she did not find the opportunity to tell Dusty her secret and knew the following day he would be too busy with running the roundup to want extra troubles on his plate. She decided to wait and see if Scales' mysterious client made any further moves against her before she bothered Dusty with her troubles.

CHAPTER SEVEN

Start The Circle, Bring Them In!

Dawn found men gathered at Dusty's appointed spot. Already the cooks had fires going and coffee pots steamed and bubbled. Each ranch had sent its quota of men to help with the work and the Lazy N's full crew were present, for this was their home range.

Although the other ranch crews for the most part steered clear of Chisum's Long Rail hard-cases, there was none of the standing in separate, watchful groups as when they met in the Juno Saloon on Saturday. Then each ranch had been on the alert for a slight to their brand's reputation or watching to ensure that they received their just due. Now they had a roundup captain they admired and one all knew would play fair with them. So they mingled, talking, trying to drink scalding hot coffee and all eager to make a start on the roundup. In the background the various ranch remudas were held and waiting for the cowhands to select horses and start work.

"Straw bosses!" Dusty called, swinging from his paint's saddle.

Dusty noted that Curly and the other two hard-cases were among the Long Rail men and wondered why Chisum sent them along. One thing was for sure, he would have to watch that trio, for he could not see them forgetting or forgiving the licking he handed to them. Maybe one of them knew something about Candy's near-accident. No, the man that he saw walking away from the buggy had not been one of the trio or Dusty would have recognized him. Anyhow this was no time to be thinking about Candy, there was too much to do.

Half-a-dozen men, including John Poe, Jesse Evans, Greg Haslett and Saul Bunyon, gathered before Dusty. They were his lieutenants and would take charge of the sections of men. Quickly Dusty told each man how many men he would have under him, dividing the labor force evenly and with men from each branch represented in every group.

"You'll take turn about in riding outer and inner circle and working the gather at the holding spot," Dusty told them. "John, Greg, Saul, you'll work the outer circle today. Jesse, I want you and Dan here to ride inner circle. Peter, your boys can handle the holding spot. I'll have two crews on it tomorrow, but I'm not keeping men around camp for the bit of work you'll get today."

A chuckle ran through the ranks of the assembled men. It looked like Cap'n Fog aimed to keep them on the hop. Even before the chuckles ended, the straw bosses gathered their teams and told the riders their duties. Once knowing what they would be expected to do, the cowhands headed for their remudas to select the best horse of their mount—no Texan used the word string—for the work at hand.

The men on the outer circle, riding the extreme limits of the territory to be worked, picked horses which would eat miles although not animals which would be suitable for more skilled tasks. Those on the inner circle could take their younger horses, animals without the staying power, or not yet built up to the condition of hardness necessary for outer circle work. On the first morning as Dusty remarked, there would be little enough for the holding spot gang to do. When the cattle came in, it would fall on the men at the bunch ground to cut the gather, split it into the various ranch groups, brand the calves and mavericks and help make a count of the beef brought in.

Nobody wasted any time, not even the Long Rail men who were used to working at much more leisurely pace. Dusty watched men collect their horses then removed his hat, swinging it over his head.

"Start the circle, bring them in!" he yelled.

Standing by his paint, Dusty watched the scattering of the riders. Each straw boss led his men off in the desired direction and in a few moments only the cooks and such remained on the spot. Mark had ridden out with Bunyon's section so as to see something of the lie of the land. After that morning, as segundo, Mark would be too busy with the gather to do much circle riding but he intended to get out and see how Bunyon handled things. Waco went with Haslett's section, but he rode as a hand with no special privileges because he happened to be one of the OD Connected hands. The Ysabel Kid was to stay around the gather area, acting as messenger and scout should either be needed. In making that decision Dusty had Chisum in mind, for he could not see the Cattle King giving up whatever plans he might have had so easily.

"What about me, Dusty?" Naylor asked, riding up.

"Got your pencils and tally book?"

"I've a pocket full of sharpened pencils and a brand new tally book in my saddle pouch, and I'm r'aring to go."

"Then go, and take the chuck wagons with you. Lon!"

"Yo!" came the Kid's reply.

"Head the remudas to the camp ground."

"It's done."

Chuck wagons and remudas were started off across the range at a good speed. By noon the first of the cattle would be in the holding ground and the hands needing food. Happen they did not want their hides blistering off, the cooks had best make sure nobody was kept waiting for a meal. The wranglers too knew what was likely to happen should a man come in for a change of horses and not find the remuda on hand. Life was going to be a whole heap easier for all concerned happen they performed their work properly and did not give their roundup captain any cause to complain.

While riding across the range with Bunyon's party, Mark Counter took time out to study the other men assigned to work with the rancher. He only recognized two of them, although he had probably seen the others in town on the day he arrived. The two Mark knew were Walker and Gordon, Curly's helpers in the abortive attempt at proving that Dusty was not a suitable man to run the roundup. Apart from the Long Rail men, Mark could see nothing wrong with Bunyon's party, for all looked to be competent cowhands.

Bunyon appeared to know the range well enough and as they approached the Black Fork of the Brazos River, which formed the eastern boundary of the Comanche Range. The rancher halted his men and told them off in pairs, selecting a couple of the Lazy N hands to be his lead-drive men. Bunyon sent them off along the river. His choice met with Mark's unspoken approval, for the Lazy N pair knew this range and would be best able to find the point where the next group of riders' section began. The other men, working in pairs, formed a broken chain between Bunyon and the lead-drive men who in turn connected with the next group and so on until the whole party formed a vast circle with the holding ground at its center.

Before the other men could leave to take their places in the circle, there was an interruption. One of the

Bradded D's men had been told to ride with Walker and looked at the Long Rail hand.

"Hope you know this section, Walker," he said.

"Can't say as I do. Don't you?"

"Never been down this way."

"You'd best let Walker ride with me, Bunyon," Gordon suggested. "I know this section. Anyways, I don't trust this hoss of mine."

There was nothing unusual about the incident. While riding the outer circle it was advisable to make sure that at least one of each pair knew the section they worked to ensure that all the cattle hiding-places were thoroughly searched; and if a man rode an untrustworthy horse, he liked to have one of his friends, who had a reliable mount, along with him.

"Go to it then." Bunyon answered. "Let's start working."

Watching the two Long Rail men ride off, Mark felt vaguely uneasy. Years of riding danger trails had given Mark an instinct for trouble and he felt the old sensations coming to him as he watched Gordon and Walker following the rest of the group to take their place in the roundup circle. Those two men rode for Chisum, which same was good enough reason for Mark to mistrust them. However, he could not countermand Bunyon's orders or ask the rancher to revise his decision; to do so would imply a lack of faith in Bunyon's ability and ruin the cowhands' faith in their straw boss.

For all his concern, Mark could not say he saw anything wrong in the way Gordon and Walker handled themselves. Neither as much as looked back and on reaching their starting point turned their horses towards the center of the circle then waited for Bunyon to give the order to start the gather. A ringing cowhand yell from the right told that the next group's lead-drive men were in position and in a few minutes Bunyon's own lead-drive group announced they had reached their place. Pointing their horses towards the holding ground in the center of their circle, all the men started riding inwards. They did not try to keep in a rigid line, the very nature of the range country prevented that. Instead they all headed inwards at an easy pace, every man keeping his eyes open for signs of cattle, or scouring the range ahead for places where cattle might lie up.

Rounding up cattle on the open range was hard, exacting and risky work which demanded much from both men and horses. While the animal used for riding the outer circle did not need the superb skill and training of a cutting horse, it still had to be agile and fast on its feet. Often the cattle did not wish to be drifted out of a comfortable location, which same could be tricky and dangerous. The cattle were not eastern-bred bossies, nor even the white-faced Hereford stock that eventually became the standard beef animal from Canada to the Rio Grande. No sir, the animal which roamed the Texas range was none of those mild, easily-handled breeds. It was the longhorn, lean, powerful, tough, at best only half-domesticated, fast on its feet, aggressive—the bulls carried horns of up to a six foot spread—and fearing a man only while he sat on a horse.

To flush longhorns out of thick brush or off good grazing took riding skill, a fair piece of knowledge and not a little nerve. Given the right set of circumstances the longhorn, especially a bull, might forget its fear of mounted men—and then things could become mighty exciting.

"Over there," Mark said, pointing to where a flash of foxy-red color showed among the bushes to his right.

"Let's take 'em," Bunyon replied.

Swinging their horses, the two men rode through a clump of scrub oaks and pushed out a small herd of cows and calves. One of the cows swung around to try and break back for cover, but Mark's bloodbay turned her back to the rest of the bunch. Once clear of the scrub oaks, the cattle gave little or no trouble and moved ahead of the two men.

Similar scenes were taking place all through the vast circle around the holding ground as the roundup crew began to scour the range and gather in the cattle. One pair working with John Poe's group stirred out a herd of wapiti, but let the big deerlike creatures break back past them, for they had more important things on their mind than elk-hunting. In another area a large bunch of pronghorn antelope rushed through a gathered bunch, causing much profanity and some hard riding to prevent the cattle from scattering. Yet despite all the interruptions and diversions the cow-hands searched the range and the number of animals ahead of each pair of men grew larger all the time.

As they drew closer to the holding ground, the men naturally came nearer to each other. On his left side Mark could see the two Long Rail hard-cases. From the number of cattle ahead of them, the men had not been slack in their work.

Noon came and went by with the men still carrying on with their searching. Soon they would be in the area already cleared by the inner circle hands and none of the outer circle crews would be sorry, for they had enough cattle ahead of them without gathering many more. That was the reason for having an inner circle, to clear the range around the holding ground and allow the outer circle men to handle their gather which had grown to a considerable size by that time. By now the Long Rail men rode about two hundred yard to Mark's left and over to his right, about the same distance away, were the lead-drive men of the next group.

"Should be on the inner circle soon," Bunyon remarked, mopping his face with a bandana and then sending his horse leaping forward to end a roan steer's intention of heading back to the open range.

"Won't be sorry," Mark answered, performing a similar service with a brindled cow and her calf.

Ahead of them the ground dropped into a small valley with fairly clear, gently sloping sides and a thickly bush-covered bottom.

"Looks like a likely spot," Bunyon remarked. "I'll prospect it, Mark, if you can handle the gather."

"Go to it."

"I'll cut through fast and see if I can scare anything out."

"Sure, Saul, watch yourself down there."

"Won't I though?" grinned the rancher.

An area like the valley would be an ideal spot for cattle to make a home and as such must be checked out. It offered shelter from the elements, food and a place to lie up undetected by enemies. However, there was always the danger that something other than cattle might have taken over the valley for a home. The western edge of the Panhandle was part of the Texas branch of the flat-headed grizzly bear family's range and *Ursus Texensis Texensis* often denned up in a spot like the bottom of the valley. Happen a man rode in on a grizzly down there, something was likely to get hurt—that something most likely would not be the bear. Black bear also had a liking for such a spot and, while not as large, powerful, or dangerous as a grizzly, could make things mighty hectic for anybody who came unexpectedly on one in a place like the valley bottom. While the medium-sized Texan grey wolf, or the large, greyish-colored Texas cougar were not over-dangerous to man under normal conditions, they too might make bad trouble should they be met with in a den area.

Mark watched Bunyon head down into the valley, then had to give his full attention to their gather. One thing was for sure, good cowhand though he might be, he could not hold the gather together single-handed with that tempting-looking valley below calling the cattle to break for its shelter. Twisting in his saddle, Mark gave a ringing yell which brought Gordon and Walker's eyes to him. They were out on more open country and one of them could handle their gather. Reading Mark's signal correctly, Gordon gave a confirmatory wave and swung his horse towards the blond giant ready to lend a helping hand. Even before the Long Rail man arrived, Mark had to cut along the side of the gather to turn back a steer that wanted to avoid being taken in.

At the bottom of the valley Bunyon pushed his horse along through the bushes. He was not as alert as he might have been and had covered half the length of the valley before an uneasy feeling that all was not well struck him. There should have been some sign of cattle before that time, yet he had seen none. However, he had seen nothing to indicate that a large and dangerous predator made its home in the valley either, so carried on though wanting to get back and help Mark.

One of the steers in Mark's gather swung away from the others just as he signaled to the Long Rail pair. It was a big *sabina*, a red and white splotched animal probably lost from some South Texas herd, and went bouncing down the slope. Even without needing any commands, Mark's big bloodbay stallion shot forward. Having learned the futility of resisting the will of a man on a horse, the *sabina* turned back to the gather, but Mark did not follow it.

Just as Mark was about to swing the bloodbay back to the gather, he saw a movement in the bushes some distance behind Bunyon. Like the rancher, Mark had been puzzled by the lack of cattle in the valley bottom. Now he saw the cause of the deficiency—and also saw that Bunyon had found himself some bad trouble.

A huge black longhorn bull burst from the center of a thick clump of bushes where it had been lying up. With head lowered, the bull hurled itself along the bottom of the valley after the rancher; and it went like it meant mischief. Either an injury, old age, or just higher than usual longhorn cussedness caused the bull to become a loner. It had moved into the valley and established itself as sole and undisputed resident, so did not aim to allow even a man on a horse to invade its territory unchallenged. However, it was too smart to charge a man head-on and let him pass before attacking.

Hearing the bull's warning snort then the thunder of hooves, Bunyon started to swing his horse around. In doing so he made a mistake, forgetting that he was not afork one of his regular string. The horse he rode was ideal for the general work on the outer circle, but not as steady as it might have been. It would have taken a real steady horse to face up to the menace of that charging longhorn. Bunyon's mount took one look at the six foot spread of horns and the mean face between them and decided that it wanted no part at all of the bull. Rearing on its hind legs, the horse took off for a safer area—only it went alone. Taken by surprise by the sudden rearing of the horse, Bunyon went backwards over the cantle of his saddle and landed rump first full in the path of the charging bull.

Mark was already charging his bloodbay down the slope and the big stallion had the legs of any bull in a foot-race. Ignoring the sight of Bunyon's horse dashing up the other side of the valley, Mark urged his stallion forward until it came along the left flank of the bull. Although Mark had his Winchester in the saddle-boot and the matched Peacemakers rode their holsters, he gave no thought to drawing or using any of them. While the .44/40 loads in the rifle or the .45 bullets in his Colts would kill the bull if they hit the right spot, neither possessed the power to drop the animal in its tracks; and only by doing so could Mark hope to save the rancher's life.

If it came right down to cases, there was only one slight chance of stopping the bull before it reached and gored the fallen, winded rancher—and it was not a way most men would even have considered. Maybe not even Mark Counter, the blond giant from the Texas Big Bend, could bring if off—but he sure as hell aimed to make a try.

There was no time to jockey his horse into a perfect position, or even do more than take a quick glance to gauge the distance between the stallion and the bull. Kicking his feet free from the stirrup irons, Mark dropped sideways to the right out of his saddle and landed on the neck of the bull. Even as Mark made his move, he saw the raw, open wound in the bull's side and knew why it denned up in the valley bottom. Then he forgot the sight, for he landed on the bull. His right arm shot out, passing over the bull's neck and a hand with the grip of a steel-jawed bear-trap clamped hold of the loose bottom skin at the base of the right horn. At the same moment Mark's left hand grabbed and held the tip of the bull's left horn. As he left the saddle, Mark let all his weight land on his left elbow and twisted at the bull's neck, trying to throw it off balance and bring it to the ground. One glance ahead told Mark that he would not succeed in time.

Some folks, having seen the feat of bull-dogging performed by the star of a Bill-show, might have thought Mark to be incompetent, for the Bill-show hand did not have any trouble in bringing his critter down. However, such men performed on the open, level ground of the show's arena, using eastern-bred stock or a half-grown steer, not nine hundred and seventy-five pounds of range-wild longhorn bull. So there was a damned good excuse for Mark failing to bring down the bull on his first attempt.

Mark glanced ahead, seeing how close Bunyon was to him. The bull was not going to fall in time! It seemed that Bunyon was still too dazed by his fall to do anything useful. Dropping his feet to the ground, Mark dug his heels in, threw back all his weight and exerted his giant strength in an attempt to halt the bull in its tracks. Mark wore boots made by the El Paso leather-working master Joe Gaylin—who swore that nothing either side of hell could rip or break the heels off a pair of boots he made. If ever Gaylin's boast was put to the test, Mark did it at that moment. Using all his giant strength, Mark fought to stop the bull. He retained his hold on the animal's head, twisting it and hauling it back. With his boot heels spiked into the ground, he actually halted the bull's progress. Sweat poured down his face, while the muscles under his shirt writhed and welled up with the strain. Ample though his shirt sleeves had been made, they stretched tight over the rising of his enormous biceps and looked almost ready to burst.

Even as Mark landed on the ground, Gordon arrived at the head of the slope. Reaching down, the Long Rail man jerked out his rifle and threw it to his shoulder. He sighted quickly and fired a shot downwards. The bullet ripped through the air just over Mark's shoulder, coming so close that he felt the wind of its passing. Surprise almost caused the big Texan to lose his hold; even though he hung on, the bull managed to drag him forward. Luckily for Bunyon, the rancher had recovered enough to roll unhurriedly aside, or he would have been trampled under-foot.

"Stop that fool shooting, man!" Bunyon yelled. "Get down here and help!"

For a moment Gordon hesitated. When he first saw the scene at the foot of the slope, he had been presented with a glorious opportunity to carry out his boss's orders. If he could put lead into Mark Counter, even if he only wounded the blond giant, Mark would release his hold on the bull and leave it free to gore Bunyon. There would be no way that Gordon's story that he fired to kill the bull, but the animal dragged

Mark into the bullet's path, could be disproved. Bunyon would be either dead or badly wounded and Gordon could claim his boss's bounty.

However, Gordon saw that Bunyon's horse had
fled up the other side of the valley and into sight of
the next group's lead-drive men. One of the pair raced
his horse forward, for the sight of a saddle mount
without a rider had ever been a cause of grave concern
among western folk. The cowhand caught Bunyon's
horse and led it back towards the top of the valley
and Gordon knew his chance had slipped away. Boot-
ing his rifle, Gordon rode down the slope only to have
to swing back and take charge of Mark and Bunyon's
restless gather which, fortunately, had not broken when
he fired his rifle.

Mark suddenly gave a surging heave backwards.
The bull's head tilted up into the air, then a dull pop
sounded and the huge animal went down with its neck
broken. Releasing his hold, the big Texan staggered
a few paces to one side and Bunyon rose, shooting
out a hand to steady the blond giant.

After a few seconds Mark had regained his breath.
He looked down at the bull, then lifted his eyes to the
rancher's face. Bunyon appeared to be a mite pale
under his tan and his grin looked sickly.

"Sorry I had to do that," Mark said. "Anyways,
he was hurt bad and would've been trouble happen
we'd taken him in."

"Sure. Thanks, Mark," Bunyon replied. "I don't
want you to think I was scared—I allus wet my pants
at this time of day."

"Now us at the Walking W," put in the lead-drive
man, coming up with Bunyon's horse and surveying
the bull's body, "we allus fetches 'em in alive. Here,
Saul, what happened, lose your hat and get off to look
for it?"

A grin creased Mark's face as the cowhand suggested the old excuse sometimes given when a man

had lost his horse. Then the grin died and Mark looked up the slope to where the Long Rail man handled their gather.

"Did he do the shooting?"

"Sure, Mark?" Bunyon replied. "Reckon he figgered to help."

"He near on did it, too. I almost lost my hold when the bullet hissed by my head. Come on, let's get moving."

On the face of it, Gordon might well have been trying to help Mark, even if acting a mite thoughtlessly. For all that, Mark decided to keep a close watch on the activities of the Long Rail man.

CHAPTER EIGHT

Three Kings Don't Lick a Straight

Long before the outer circle men came into sight of the holding ground, they could see the smoke of several fires rising into the air. Topping a rim, Mark drew rein for a moment to look at a familiar, yet always fascinating scene. On the large open plain bordering a stream lay the holding ground. From all appearances the inner circle men had also made a good gather, and already the hands were at work cutting cattle from it. From two other points large bands of cattle were being driven in to join the main herd. Off to the north of the holding ground, also on the banks of the stream, the ranches' remudas grazed under the watchful eyes of the wranglers, beyond them the cooks had set up camp.

"The inner circle gathered well, Mark," Bunyon remarked as the blond giant started his horse forward once more. "If all the ranges show as well as this, we won't have lost much stock over winter."

"Looks that way, Saul. Say, get a man up here at the point with you. I want to head on in and see if Dusty's got anything for me to do."

"Reckon he will have have?"

"Time he hasn't, I'll be surprised."

With that Mark left the cattle and rode forward at a better speed towards the holding ground. One of the other hands came forward and took Mark's place at the point of their gather, steering the cattle down towards the branding fires.

Dusty turned as his big *amigo* rode up.

"That's a fair-sized *petalta* you've got there, Dusty," Mark said, using the South Texas term for a herd gathered to be cut on a roundup.

"We've had our moments," Dusty answered with a grin. "Banker Goadby came out from town, allowed to see how safe his bank loans were. I've got him handling a second tally book. How'd Bunyon shape out?"

"He'll do."

"Huh huh," Dusty grunted, then looked to where Waco came racing up from Haslett's party.

"Done done my share, Cap'n sir," the youngster said.

"Have, huh?"

"Done as done, which same's done enough."

"Lon's branding over there," Dusty said. "He's been yelling 'More straw' for the past hour. Go flank for him."

"Me?" yelped Waco.

"I know that paint's one smart horse, boy; but me 'n' Mark's never seen *it* flank down calves."

"That'll teach you to talk, boy," grinned Mark.

Mark ought to have known better than attract attention to himself. Turning, Dusty looked at his big *amigo*.

"Take the boy back to camp, grab a meal, then come and cut some out for him to flank."

"Sure thing. I've been wanting to see if that pair of cutting horses I borrowed from Colonel Charlie are as good as he reckoned."

Leaving Dusty, Mark and Waco headed north along

the bank of the stream. They tended to their horses, changed saddles on to fresh mounts and then rode on to the camp where the cooks had a meal waiting for the men who came in from the outer circle. Once fed, the two friends wasted no time in heading back towards the herd. Waco rode one of the horses given him as a string for the foreman of the JA and Mark sat a red-gold colored California sorrel which Goodnight had sworn was a cutting horse of the finest water and well up to carrying the blond giant's weight.

Back at the *petalta* Waco left his horse standing with its reins dangling and drew on a pair of leather gauntlets ready to start flanking down calves brought to the fire by the ropers. The Ysabel Kid was just thrusting a branding iron's head into the fire and gave the time-honored bellow of, "More straw!"—which did not mean more fuel for the fire, but that he wanted more animals to brand.

Despite his two hundred and ten pounds weight, Mark rode light in the saddle and took less out of his horse than would a less skillful if not so heavy man. On his way from the wagons Mark had got the feel of the sorrel and let the animal know it had a good rider on its back. He reckoned they would work well together, so headed the sorrel towards the *petalta*.

A cow with a calf at its side caught Mark's eye and he headed towards it, seeing the Lazy N brand the cow carried. After showing the sorrel the cow he wanted Mark sat back and let the horse do the rest. He soon found that Goodnight's boast had been true. Working quietly and without any fuss, with the minimum guidance from Mark, the sorrel edged the cow, followed by its calf, from the herd. Once clear, the cow showed a desire to get back among her friends, but each time the fast moving sorrel spun before her and blocked her way. All Mark needed to do while this went on was anticipate the sorrel's twists and turns so as to stay in the saddle.

"Lazy N!" Mark yelled as a roper rode up and dropped his loop on the calf. "Tally one and one!"

By the fire Naylor, the tally man, made a mark in the appropriate columns of his thumb-marked book to show a further cow and calf of his brand had been cut out of the herd. Most of the animals brought in so far had been Lazy N or JA stock, although a fair amount of grown mavericks were gathered to one side and a few branded animals from southern range spreads had been removed from the *petalta*.

Dragging the protesting calf after him, the roper headed towards where Waco stood waiting. Mark's cutting horse now had the task of holding back the cow and preventing her from charging down in defense of her offspring. As the calf came up, Waco watched his chance. Shooting his left hand over the calf's neck, he grabbed hold of the rope close to the animal's neck. Waco's right hand also passed over the calf's back to grab the flank. Jerking up with his hands and thrusting out with his right knee, Waco swung the calf's legs from under it and away from him. He dumped the calf side down and held it on the ground, then looked towards the fire.

"Calf on the ground!" he yelled.

At the branding fire the Ysabel Kid lifted one of the heating Lazy N branding irons. He glanced at the head to make sure it was glowing a cherry-red with the heat. Giving the iron's rod a bang on his forearm to knock off any burning particles of wood which might adhere to it, the Kid walked towards the calf. Quickly and surely he placed the iron's head against the animal's side. Smoke rose and the stench of burning hair and flesh rose into the air. The calf let out a bleat of pain and only the superb skill of the cutting horse prevented its mother getting by and at the branding crew. Jerking the rope from the calf's neck, Waco set the little animal free. It lurched to its feet and headed back to its mother as fast as it could go. Mark

drove the cow and calf to the Lazy N's bunch and
left them in the care of the ranch's rep, then headed
back to the herd.

The work continued as other men did their part in
cutting the herd. Each local ranch had one man along
as their representative. His main task was to gather
and tend to his own spread's cattle after they were cut
from the *petalta* and to identify himself he wore a
"blab board", a square of leather bearing the brand of
his outfit, suspended around his neck. The job was
one of importance and the tophand of the spread handled it. When he had gathered all his spread's stock
that he could handle, he would haze them back on to
his own range and put them in a location they would
be unlikely to leave, remembering it to warn the
roundup crew so the stock would not be gathered and
counted twice.

Not until the sun started to sink in the west did
Dusty call a halt to the work. He had sent several men
to the wagons earlier and they returned to take over
as night herd with the task of holding the *petalta*
together and keeping the other groups of cut cattle
separate from each other.

Only when all the guards were on their patrols did
Dusty leave the herd and head for the camp. The first
thing he saw was that several people from the town
had come out to the herd, Candy Carde among them.
However, before he could speak to the girl, Dusty
found the ranchers waiting for him.

"It went down real well today, Cap'n," Sanders of
the Box S said as the men gathered around their roundup
captain.

"We've a long way to go," Dusty answered.

"How's about them mavericks, Cap'n?" asked
Chisum. "Reckon we ought to cut 'em among us each
day?"

There were several unbranded animals already cut
from the herd, but hardly enough to be shared out.

However, Dusty decided to wait to hear what the other men wanted to do before saying anything. Once more, as had happened at the meeting in town, the ranchers went the opposite way to Chisum.

"I'd say leave 'em for a week at least, make it worth our while to split 'em," Meadows of the Flying M stated and a rumble of agreement went up from most of the other ranchers.

"That's what I'd've suggested," Dusty agreed. "If we've enough to make it worth our while, we'll cut the mavericks among the ranches on Monday morning."

"Have you enough men?" Naylor inquired.

"Took on half-a-dozen today, Jim."

None of the ranchers raised any objections to Dusty's words, nor felt surprised to hear that cowhands had drifted up looking for work. The mysterious, but highly effective, prairie-telegraph had passed out word of the forthcoming roundup and cowhands who were out of a job, or just wanted a change of scenery and faces, came looking for work.

"Some of my boys aim to go into town if it's all right, Cap'n," Meadows went on.

"Are they on night herd?"

"Nope."

"They're men-grown, I can't stop them. Only make sure they know that we're starting good and early in the morning."

"I'll warn 'em," Meadows grinned. "Anyways, they cain't get roostered, not with pay day two days gone by."

The Flying M was one of the furthest north spreads and its hands did not often have a chance to visit a town more than once a month. However, Dusty knew the trouble a bunch of drunken cowhands could cause in a roundup camp. With everybody working hard for long hours in the day-time, tempers were inclined to rise should their sleep be disturbed at night. Still Dusty had no right to refuse the cowhands a chance to go into town and if, as Meadows claimed, the hands did not have much money, they would not be likely to get into trouble.

Candy had been watching the meeting with growing impatience. Setting her feet down in grim, determined steps, she headed towards the men and interrupted as Dickens, who had eaten earlier, prepared to raise some other point for Dusty's attention.

"Come on, boys," she said. "Let's let Captain Fog have a meal, shall we?"

Her words had the desired effect in that they broke up the meeting. The ranchers realized that Dusty had not yet managed to get a meal and so split up to return to their wives or their ranch crews.

"Thanks, Candy," Dusty said with a grin.

"Why thank me, I haven't had a chance to speak to you all afternoon. Come on, I'll get you some food."

The Four Flying M hands happened to pass Dusty's party on their way to the remuda. All were young men, hard-working, loyal to their brand, but tended to be a mite wild and irresponsible, so Dusty decided a warning would not be out of place.

"Hey, you Flying M's," he called.

"Sure, Cap'n?"

"Don't make too much noise coming back. There'll be folks asleep."

"And cows, too," Mark went on, "and you know how they get happen they're woken up in the night."

"We'll be good and quiet," promised the spokesman for the quartet. "Won't we, boys?"

"Way our money's fixed, we'll have to be," grinned another. "Unless Miss Candy'll give us credit."

"You know my motto, boys," the girl answered, "In the Lord I trust, mortals pay cash."

All four laughed, knowing that Candy would loan them some money if they needed it urgently. She

would not loan them any just so they could have a
few extra drinks in town.

The words had carried to where Lawyer Scales
stood with the Naylors and a couple of town businessmen. A calculating glint came into his eyes as he
looked in the direction of the four departing cowhands.

"I think I'll be getting back to town," he said,
giving a yawn. "All this fresh air's no good for city
boys like me."

While she wondered what was taking Scales away
in such a hurry, Laura Naylor raised no objections.
Watching Scales walk away, Laura wondered why he
was so eager to help her persuade her husband to sell
the ranch. The lawyer had visited her that morning
and yet had not made any suggestions about how she
could get her husband to sell out and take her back
East.

Collecting his horse, Scales rode back to town in
the wake of the four Flying M hands. At his home,
he entered his bedroom, made sure that the window's
curtains were drawn together and that nobody could
see inside, then unlocked and opened a trunk he took
from under his bed.

Back at the camp, the Ysabel Kid discovered that
he had no tobacco; which promptly persuaded Dusty,
Mark and Waco that they had also run out.

"Huh, white-eye brothers plenty mean with-um
makings," grunted the Kid in his best Comanche Dog
Soldier voice. "You-all mean you'd let poor lil ole
me ride all that way into town to buy some?"

"We sure would," agreed three voices.

"Just to make up for them all being so mean to
you, Lon," Candy put in, "you can escort me in."

"Gee, thanks, Candy, you all restored my faith in
the white-eye brother."

"Me, a *brother?*"

"Lon's lived a sheltered life," Mark drawled. "I'll

go check the night herd and see everything's all right, Dusty."

"And you go collect the lady's buggy, boy," the Kid drawled, "while I get my old Blackie hoss."

"I'll do that," Waco agreed, wondering if he would ever grow old enough to stop being the "boy" to the three men he would have died for and deciding, as he always did, that he had no objection to the name as long as they used it. "Want for me to fetch Candy's buggy along too?"

For a moment Candy did not catch the drift of Waco's remark; and when she did he was out of throwing range. Turning to Dusty, she laughed merrily.

"That's quite a boy," she said. "I wish you were riding in with me, Dustine."

"So do I, Candy. But I have to stay on out here and take care of things. But you just wait until after the roundup—"

"And then what?"

"Just you wait and see."

Which was all Candy could get out of him on the matter. She looked at Dusty for a moment, then smiled. Unless she was sadly mistaken, it would be worth waiting for.

The Kid escorted Candy across the range, following the trail into town. At one point they had to pass through a small wood, but it was silent and deserted after being cleaned out by the roundup crew that afternoon. The girl spend most of the ride asking questions and learning about Dusty Fog.

On arriving at the Juno Saloon, Candy left the Kid while she went to her rooms and changed into her working clothes. There was a small crowd of customers, mostly townsmen, although with a few cowhands from the southern ranches below the Comanche range. At the bar, the Kid looked around the room and saw the four Flying M hands playing poker with a dude. There was something vaguely familiar about the dude, yet the Kid could not remember having seen the man around town since his arrival on Saturday. Not that one would easily forget the dude. He wore a loud check suit, a white shirt and fancy bow tie of Eastern style and had gloves on his hands. A grey derby hat perched on a head of shaggy black hair and the man's spectacles, moustache and bushy beard prevented much of his face showing.

"Who's the jasper with the fancy suit?" the Kid asked the bartender who brought him a glass of beer.

"Never saw him afore, looks like a drummer of some sort to me. He come in, bought a drink and then went over to join the Flying M in a card game."

"Reckon he's a card-shark?"

"If he is, he'll sure be picking slim there," grinned the bartender. "I gave Rocky five bucks on his gun, which same made him rich man of the party."

"Looks like Rocky's hit a lucky streak then," the Kid replied, watching the spokesman for the quartet rake in a handful of dollar bills from the pot.

At the moment Rocky became aware of the Kid's presence and turned in his chair to wave and yell.

"Hey, Kid! Come on over and take a drink."

Leaving the bar, the Kid crossed to the Flying M's table and accepted a glass of whisky from Rocky. There was not much money on the table and all the Kid could see looked to be one dollar bills. If the dude was a card-shark, he did not seem likely to make eating money out of the cowhands. While sipping at his drink, the Kid studied the dude again, sure he had seen the man before and wondering where, Rocky introduced the man as a clothing drummer, salesman, and by his first name. Watching the dude riffle the deck of cards, the Kid saw none of the feather-fingered skill of a professional gambler. Nor, when the man started dealing, did the Kid see any sign of him handling the deck in the manner of a professional cheat.

"Sitting in, Kid?" Rocky asked.

"Game's too high for me," answered the Kid,

glancing to where Candy came down the stairs. "See you later, boys."

"Don't do nothing we wouldn't," grinned one of the cowhands.

"Which same gives you plenty of scope," Rocky went on.

Turning, the Kid joined Candy at the bar. At the table the dude finished dealing and cards were raised. The betting became brisk and the hand offered the largest pot of the night. There must have been over thirty dollars in it, almost a months pay for a cowhand, when the dude called Rocky's final bet.

"Three lil kings," grinned the cowhand.

"Licks me," replied the dude and shoved back his chair. "That's all for me tonight, boys. I've got an early start in the morning."

"How's about taking a drink afore you go?" Rocky asked, conscious of his duty as the game's big winner.

"Not tonight, thanks,"

"Shucks, the night's young, ain't it, boys?"

"The night might be," grinned the drummer in a disarming tone, "but I'm not any more. You fellers don't let me spoil your fun none."

"Come on, Rocky," whooped one of the Flying M hands. "We got some drinking to catch up on."

Led by Rocky, the Flying M hands headed for the bar, their faces flushed with delight at having won enough money to pay for a celebration. The drummer rose and walked across the room, passing through the batwing doors and out of sight.

"It looks like Rocky and the others made a kill," Candy remarked to the Kid.

"Sure, and you're going to get most of it over the bar."

"Yes," the girl admitted, not sounding any too pleased at the thought of having some extra trade. "Put money in Rocky's pocket, and it burns holes until he spends it."

"He's a cowhand," replied the Kid.

"He's a noisy young cuss when he's liquored up," Candy answered. "I'll go collect the cards, everybody else seems to be busy."

Crossing the room, Candy started to gather up the discarded cards. In doing so she turned over the drummer's losing hand and glanced down at it. A frown came to her face and she placed the five cards on the bottom of the deck, then walked back to the bar where the four cowhands had gathered around the Kid.

"I sure showed him," Rocky was saying as Candy came up. "Three lil ole kings of mine licked him good."

"Three kings?" Candy asked.

"Sure, Miss Candy, ma'am. All of 'em but the lil king of clubs. Say, would you-all do us the honor of having a drink?"

"Not right now, Rocky, thanks. I've got some work to do. Aren't you boys due back at camp soon?"

"Us, ma'am?" grinned Rocky. "Shuckens, no. Ain't got a thing to do afore morning and we got money in our pocket. This's our night to howl."

"Looks that way," Candy smiled and turned to the Kid. "Can I see you, Kid?"

"Just look under the hat, I'm there someplace," he replied and left the Flying M boys pouring out drinks. "You all look a mite worried, Candy."

"How'd that drummer who lost the money strike you, Kid—and don't say he never laid a hand on you."

"Shucks, now you went and spoiled it for me. How'd you mean, strike me?"

"Did he look like he knew how to play poker?" Candy asked.

"Why sure. He looked that way from what I saw."

"Rocky won the last pot with three kings, didn't he?"

"Yep."

"Three kings don't lick a straight."

"So they tell me," drawled the Kid, then looked

at the deck of cards in Candy's hands.

Slowly Candy turned over the deck and exposed the bottom five cards; they were seven and eight of clubs, nine of hearts, ten of diamonds and jack of spades.

"You mean that was his hand?" asked the Kid.

"My, don't tell me you thought that out all by yourself?" she answered.

"Pale-face squaw got-um more lip than a muley cow," the Kid grunted. "Say, where'd that dude be likely to stop in town?"

"Mrs. Tappley takes in roomers, that would be the most likely place," Candy replied. "What's wrong, Kid?"

"I've got a suspicious mind."

"It comes of being a border smuggler."

"I treat that remark with the contempt it deserves, ma'am," the Kid told Candy severely, doffed his hat in a gallant flourish and left the saloon.

First he called at Mrs. Tappley's home but the lady disclaimed all knowledge of the drummer. She did suggest a couple of other places where the man might be staying and the Kid visited them, then called in at the livery barn and finally went to the Wells Fargo office where he found one of the clerks still working.

On his return to the Juno, the Kid found that the Flying M boys were well on their way to getting drunk and making plenty of noise with it. Candy crossed the room and joined the Kid.

"Well?" she said.

"That feller's not in town and never came, way I've heard it," replied the Kid. "He's not staying any place in town, didn't come in on a stage or a hoss. I checked at both the livery barn and the stage office."

"But we saw him," Candy objected.

"Why sure. I know that's tolerable powerful likker you serve, Candy, but it only affects man after he's drunk it."

"He couldn't have walked in. Maybe he came by

small wagon and left it outside the town limits."

"Maybe, but I don't buy it. Say, what're those Flying M boys like when they're in likker?"

"Noisy," Candy replied. "Harmless, thoughtless and real noisy. They're getting that way now."

"Like whooping things up, huh?"

"Listen to them."

"I am listening," drawled the Kid.

"Are you going to stop them?" asked Candy, watching Rocky pour out drinks for his friends and four of her girls.

"Reckon I could?"

"My boys would help you."

The Kid shook his head. Having more than a little experience of the working of cowhand mentality, he knew that any attempt at stopping the four youngsters enjoying themselves must lead to trouble. There was a better way to handle the matter, happen he remembered the lay of the land correctly.

"I'm headed back to camp, Candy," he said.

"But what about them?" she asked.

"Let'em have their fling."

"And if they go back to camp raising their usual fuss?"

A grin split the Kid's face, making him look very young and as innocent as a church-pew full-loaded with choirboys.

"Happen they do," he said, "I'll put a Comanche curse on them."

Candy frowned as she watched the Kid walk from the saloon. If it had been anybody but one of Dusty's three *amigos* she might have followed him and tried to make him take some positive action. Should Rocky and his friends return to the camp in their usual rowdy way, they might easily spook the gathered cattle and scatter them across the range. Not that they would do so intentionally, but when they had a belly-full of Old Stump Blaster they just did not think of what their actions might bring about. Yet the Kid knew the danger as well as, if not even better, than Candy and she could not understand his casual attitude.

Turning back to the bar, Candy caught the attention of her bartender and he walked along to join her. Her questions about the identity of the drummer met with no result; the bartender said he had never seen the man before and could not guess where the drummer came from. A puzzled and worried Candy stood watching the Flying M quartet continue their celebration. Not until all the money they had won went over the bar top did they leave the saloon. Candy stood at the door and watched the whooping, yelling quartet ride out of town. If they reached the herd still making so much noise, and she did not doubt but that they would, the four cowhands could spoil all Dusty's work and make endless trouble for their boss. The other ranchers would not take Rocky and his friends' actions lightly should a day's hard work go for nothing through the drunken folly of the Flying M hands.

Making almost enough racket to wake the dead, and holding their horses to a fast lope, Rocky and his three *amigos* rode into the wood about a mile from town and a good three miles from their camp.

"Bet they're all asleep back to camp," one of the quartet whooped.

"We'll waken 'em when we get there," Rocky answered. "Yahoo! When we don't sleep nobody sleeps."

"Scatter 'em, Flyi—!" began the youngster at Rocky's right.

The words ended as Rocky suddenly jerked backwards over the cantle of his saddle. Before the speaker could wonder at the phenomenon, something caught his chest and hooked him back off his horse. The other two cowhands, following close on the first pair's heels, were too drunk to react quickly and the rope stretched across the trail at just the right height stopped their forward progress, although it did not stop their horses, sweeping the cowhands from their saddles. All four crashed down in a surprised, cursing heap and their horses went tearing off along the path through the trees.

Standing at one end of the rope, the Ysabel Kid jerked it free of the tree to which it was tied. He bounded on silent feet across the path some ten feet ahead of the still yelling, cursing hands. The black clothing merged with the darkness of the path and the Kid reached the other side unseen. Quickly he freed the other end of his rope, having put it in place when he heard the noise of the approaching party. Coiling the ropes as he went, the Kid glided off through the trees. His big white stallion stood like a statue, waiting for him and he went afork it in a single bound. The four Flying M horses were slowing down on the open land beyond the wood when the Kid caught up with them. Collecting the reins, he led their four horses across the range towards the roundup camp.

"What happened?" asked the Flying M's night hawk as the Kid rode up.

The Kid told what had happened in town and the night hawk, a leathery old-timer who had committed most of the cowhand follies himself in his time, gave a chuckle as he listened. He could see the danger Rocky's quartet presented to the herd and reckoned they deserved a lesson.

"I'll go back and watch 'em in," the Kid drawled, "only they won't know I'm doing it."

There were dangers to men on foot and the Kid did not want Rocky's party to sustain any injury through his setting them afoot.

"Sure. I'll take their saddles into camp for 'em. Allus allow they strayed in, the hosses I mean," grinned the night hawk. "Boy, I bets young Rocky and the others don't feel like going celebrating again for a spell after walking back from town. Bet they're all sobered up when they get here, too."

CHAPTER NINE

Start Shooting As Soon As You Like

The night hawk's prediction proved to be correct. Around two o'clock in the morning a disgruntled, sober and silent quartet of cowboys hobbled into camp. Cowhand boots had never been designed for long-distance walking and all four young men's feet ached as they reached the camp. Not one of the quartet had any idea how they came to the lose their horses and all swore they would never touch another drink as long as they lived.

At the first light of day the cooks roused out the camp. Rocky and his three friends, all showing signs of being hungover, crawled out of their blankets to join the rest of the roundup crew in collecting breakfast.

"Reckon they're cured," drawled Dusty, watching the Flying M quartet limp by where he stood with his three *amigos* and ate his breakfast. "I bet you couldn't get them to go to town again after last night—not for a few days anyway."

"There's something about what happened last night that I don't like, Dusty," Mark said.

"And me," agreed Waco. "Why should that drummer let Rocky and the others win money off him?"

"Maybe he wanted company," Dusty suggested.

"Didn't look to, way he pulled out so early," remarked the Kid. "And that don't tell us how he come to town in the first place."

"Man'd think the drummer wanted those boys to get drunk and come back here waking folks up," Waco drawled. "That could have started trouble if it happened. Walking W and Flying M aren't any too friendly, Rocky and his boys might have stirred trouble between the two outfits happen they'd come in whooping and yelling."

For a few seconds the four Texans ate in silence. All thought of what might have happened had the drunken quartet come in whooping and yelling. A feud in the middle of a roundup did not make for smooth working conditions; and shooting wars had started over less cause than a bunch of irresponsible cowhands scattering the gather and disturbing the camp's sleep.

"There was that business with the bull yesterday, too," Waco went on, swallowing a mouthful of beef. "Happen Gordon'd've even grazed you, you'd've let the bull go, Mark. Then Bunyon'd've got hurt bad."

"Gordon might only have been trying to help," Mark answered. "I got talking with Jesse Evans last night, Dusty. He allows that Chisum bought this land up here with the intention of getting control of all the range south until it ties on to his Long Rail in New Mexico."

"Bunyon's spread's north of Chisum's though," Dusty pointed out.

"Maybe Chisum's getting land hungry," drawled the Kid.

"Which same doesn't explain how Chisum got word to the drummer in town and set up that business with Rocky and the others," Dusty pointed out. "Come on, we're going to have to make a start. Keep your eyes peeled, all of you, I don't like the way things are going on this chore. Lon, first chance you get head into town and ask Candy to learn all she can about that drummer."

"I'll do it," replied the Kid.

There would be a change in the method of working on the second day of the round up. They had cleared most of the Naylor spread the first day and were starting to work the larger JA range. Instead of following the previous day's procedure, the gathering crews would form only half a circle, with the holding ground as its open end. Only two of the sections would be on the outer circle that day, Haslett's and Evans'; Haslett took his men to the right while Evans went to the left. They had orders to meet up on the far side of their area after laying out their men in a chain behind them.

Waco rode with Haslett's crew as he had on the previous day. He and the young rancher got on well enough and Haslett's wife had been among the visitors to the camp the night before. Waco met her, a pretty, red-haired girl who laughed and talked easily.

Among Haslett's bunch was a tall, handsome, well-dressed man called Marwood. From the start Waco took a dislike to Marwood, for the man had a cocky, swaggering self-assurance which did not go with his skill as a cowhand. Marwood had come in with the Long Rail crew and Waco suspected that the man was one of Chisum's "warriors"; which would account for his good clothes and lack of cowhand skill. On the previous day Marwood had been mocking and sneering but did not force the issue of who was boss of their group.

It happened that the men did not have to separate for a time, not until they left the area cleared out the previous day. Haslett's party rode in a bunch and talk went on among them.

"Hey, Greg," Marwood said, bringing his horse alongside the rancher's. "Who was that red-headed lil gal I saw you with last night?"

"My wife."

"No fooling? I could've sworn I'd seen her afore."

"Could, huh?" grunted Haslett coldly.

While he felt no shame at his wife having worked in a saloon, Haslett did not care to mention the fact to Marwood.

"How'd you reckon Rocky of the Flying M's horse got back to camp last night, Greg?" Waco put in, coming on the other side of the young rancher.

Over breakfast Rocky and his three pards had profanely told the story of their adventures the previous night. All expressed surprise at finding their horses in the ranch's remuda and their saddles by the Flying M's area of the camp. While a range horse would mostly find its way home should it be left riderless, the animals Rocky's bunch rode would hardly regard the roundup camp as their home. Rocky had expected that his horse and saddle would be on their way to the Flying M and had expressed his bewilderment at finding both at the camp. It said much for the Flying M night hawk's self-control that he did not give the game away. The apparent intelligence of the four horses had been the subject of much discussion around the cooking fires and several novel explanations for their behavior were put forth.

Waco's interruption served its purpose and allowed Haslett to keep up a conversation clear of his wife until they reached the edge of the cleaned area. Then he told Marwood to take the first position, but to wait for the signal before beginning his sweep.

Leaving Marwood behind, Haslett led his men on, dropping one after another off at intervals of about half a mile until he saw Jesse Evans approaching from the other direction to complete the half-circle.

"Ready, Jesse?" he yelled.

"Ready as I can be!" came the answer.

"Let's go then."

Each straw boss turned his horse towards the holding ground and let out a yell to the next man of his group who in turn passed on the signal. Once again the business of scouring the range began. Each man swung his horse backwards and forwards across his area, checking everywhere cattle might be hiding and pushing all he found ahead of him.

Waco was thoughtful as he rode his area of the circle. Since meeting and throwing his destiny in with Dusty Fog, the youngster had learned to think things out, to look into the motives behind men's actions. Something in Marwood's attitude towards Haslett worried Waco. The Long Rail man seemed to be trying to rile Haslett up for some reason. Many folks would have noticed nothing, but Waco had been raised among proddy hard-cases and could read the signs. If Marwood was not hunting for fuss with Haslett, he sure acted like he was.

The sight of a black and white cow grazing off to his right drove all thoughts of Haslett and Marwood from Waco's head. Leaving the animals he had already gathered, Waco rode slowly and without fuss towards the cow. His quiet approach did not frighten the cow and he brought his horse alongside her, looking down at her udder.

"All right, you slab-sided varmint," he said with a grin. "Where've you got it hid?"

Standing in his stirrups, Waco looked around him. He investigated two clumps of bushes and looked behind a rock. Then he headed to a clump of mesquite and among it found the cow's calf. Just as he headed the calf into the open, the cow charged him. His horse avoided the charge and he headed mother and calf to his gather, continuing driving the cattle ahead of him.

Any time a man found a solitary cow with her udder bag showing signs of having been sucked, he knew she had a calf stashed away someplace close at hand. Then all that remained to do was to gather in the cow

and calf and point them towards the holding ground
and the *petalta*.

Long before the holding ground came into sight,
Waco's gather had grown to over thirty head. Curi-
ously enough, the larger a gather the more easy it was
to handle, for the cattle found safety in numbers and
gave less trouble in trying to break back for the open
range.

When Waco came out on to fairly open land, a
thrilling panoramic scene spread itself before him. In
addition to his thirty-eight head, the other men appeared to have done well. From all sides cows, calves,
bulls, heifers and steers were trailing across the range.
There was a continuous bellowing, the sharper blatting
of calves and the deeper bugle-boom of some bull
which protested at being driven along. Dust rose into
the air as the groups and lines of cattle converged on
the holding ground like steel filings drawn to a mag-
net's pull.

On arrival at the holding ground, the day's gather
was added to the now shrunken *petalta* collected the
previous day. The branding crews had worked hard
and only a few head remained to be cut and dealt with
when the new gather arrived. Off to the south Naylor's
hands were turning their stock back on to the cleared
range and the other spreads' cut and the maverick
gather had grown larger but were still under the control
of the holding ground crew.

"Take your boys and grab a meal," Dusty ordered
when the two straw bosses reported to him. "I want
you back here in an hour."

"Yo!" Evans replied.

"We'll be here," promised Haslett.

Just as the men turned to leave the *petalta*, they
saw Waco prove himself once more to be a very capable and efficient cowhand. One of the bulls brought
in by the circle of men decided that it had seen all it
wanted of men and their ways. With the bull to think

was to act. Whirling, it shot out of the herd and headed for the open range as fast as it could go; which same was fast enough to give a hard-ridden circle horse a decent race.

Waco sent his horse leaping after the fleeing animal before any of the other circle men could move. Unstrapping his rope as he rode, Waco brought his horse alongside the racing bull from the left. Instead of tossing his rope from a distance, he came in close. Flicking his loop over the bull's horns and head, he gave the three strand, extra-hard plaited Manila rope a jerk to draw it tight around the bull's neck. Allowing the rope to drop under the bull's right hip bone and around its buttock, Waco tied the end to his saddlehorn. Then he reined his horse to the left and brought it to a halt, bracing himself for the pull. When the slack of the rope twanged tight, the bull was brought to such a sudden halt that it seemed to reverse itself in midair and lit down on its back hard enough to jar the breath out of it. Had he wished, Waco could have left his horse and hog-tied the bull's legs before it recovered. Instead he leapt down and removed his rope, then went afork his horse in a bound.

On rising, the bull staggered back into the safety of the herd. It had learned its lesson and would give no more trouble that day.

Back at camp, after finishing their meal, the subject of handling wild stock came up among the men taking advantage of their hour's break.

"You ought to have tailed that bull down, Waco," one of the men said. "I've seen fellers do it."

"Sure, so have I," Waco agreed. "Don't reckon on it myself though, it's a mite too rough on the stock."

"Sure is," Greg Haslett said. "I've seen a steer bust its horns off landing from being tailed down."

"Back down the Pecos we used to carry saw blades under our saddle skirts and cut the tips of the bad'n's horns off," a cowhand remarked.

"I've seen greasers do it in the Big Bend," another went on. "Only they ham-string the cattle too."

"Way Dusty does it is to cut holes in a burlap sack and hang it over the wild one's horns," Waco drawled. "That way he can't see more'n the ground ahead of him and he doesn't give any fuss."

"We used to rope the wild stock horn to horn with a gentler animal and let him haul the weight," Haslett told the others. "About the cruellest trick I ever saw was down in Mexico. they sewed the wild ones' eyelids together. Say one thing though, I've never known a white man to pull that trick."

None of the group had noticed Marwood standing behind them. As usual the cowhands tended to stay clear of the Long Rail hard-cases and only rarely did any of Chisum's hands join in the general conversation which went on around the fires.

"I've done it afore now," Marwood said.

All eyes turned towards the speaker and a general look of disapproval came to each face. While a cowhand's work did not tend to be humane or gentle, only a few of them practiced deliberate cruelty on their charges. Blinding a bad animal was neither pleasant, amusing nor necessary and none of the men harbored much of an opinion of a man who boasted of doing it.

"You'd best not try it while you're working under me," Haslett warned.

"Never could stand a humane boss."

There was a mocking insolence in the way Marwood sneered out his words. Every member of the listening crowd caught it and watched Greg Haslett's face, knowing the young rancher must be fully aware of the suggested challenge to his authority and wondering how he would meet it.

"And I could never stand a man who went out of his way to hurt things," Haslett said. "Especially something that couldn't hurt back."

"You've got a good point there, Greg," Waco drawled, hoping Marwood would turn the quarrel his way.

The gunman had no intention of doing so. Seeing his chance of forcing a showdown with Haslett fade off in one direction, he decided to try another. One more likely to succeed, or he had read the young rancher's character all wrong.

"Say, Greg," he said, "I just remembered where I saw your wife last. It *was* in Fort Worth. Didn't she work in the Green Clover Saloon there?"

"She did."

"Say then, I'd best ride over and see her to say howdy and talk over old times."

"Not while the roundup's on," Haslett answered. "After it's done, come on over any time and *we'll* make you welcome."

"She used to be good at making folks welcome all right. That was some wild place, the Green Clover. Has she told you about it?"

"She's told me," Haslett replied, the voice growing cold and angry.

"I bet she never told you all that happened there," grinned Marwood.

An uneasy silence fell on the crowd and all eyes stayed on the two men. It was common knowledge that Rosie Haslett had worked in saloons before she married the young rancher. However, in the West a person's past rarely influenced the way the tolerant, easy-going cowhands accepted him or her; it was how they acted at present which counted and Rosie Haslett acted in a proper manner. Since her marriage, Rosie had been well-behaved, loyal to her husband and gave no sign that she might once have been a free-and-easy saloongirl.

Waco looked around for Jesse Evans, hoping the Long Rail's segundo would be close at hand. Despite the fact that Evans worked for Chisum, Waco liked and respected him. The Long Rail's *segundo* might end this business before it came to shooting: but Evans was nowhere in sight.

"Did she ever tell you how ole King Fisher and his boys used to take over the Green Clover every pay day?" Marwood went on. "He was some man, ole King, and he sure liked redheads. Why I bet he slept with every red-headed gal in the—"

"You're a liar, Marwood!" Haslett spat out.

In the west the words "liar" and "thief" were the worst insults one man could place on another. Neither word was said in fun and when used almost always brought on gunplay.

The smile dropped from Marwood's face, leaving behind it a cold, hard, expressionless killer's mask.

"That's a hard word, Haslett," he said. "Nobody calls me a liar and lives."

There Haslett had it. The flat challenge lay before him and he felt suddenly sick and cold in his stomach. All too well Haslett was aware of his limitations as a gunfighter. He lacked the superb coordination of mind and muscle necessary to be a fast gun. At best he was only fair and on the previous day while riding to the start of their drive Marwood had proved to be far better than that.

Yet Haslett knew he had gone too far to back down. If he stepped back, he would be finished in that area. So his pride drove him to stand his ground instead of getting out of a tight spot from which he could not hope to emerge alive. He did not want to die. Only the previous evening Rosie had told him she thought they were going to have a baby. Yet he also did not want to live and have the unborn child come into the world which called its father a coward.

Slowly Haslett started to raise his right hand from his side. The other men around the fire stood silent and watchful. Everyone of them knew how little chance the young rancher had, but they were powerless to intervene. A man stood or fell on his own two feet in Texas and all around the fire knew that the man who interfered would have to face Marwood himself. Haslett's eyes stayed on Marwood's face and he read the cold confidence, the sureness of victory with which the Long Rail "warrior" regarded him. It appeared that Marwood knew Haslett did not have a chance.

"Start shooting as soon as you like," Marwood said. "I'll give you first grab."

In the absence of Jesse Evans, Waco decided that he must take action to prevent Haslett's death. Slipping the horn-handled pen-knife from his pants pocket, he opened the small blade. With the skill gained in youthful games of mumbleypeg, Waco flipped out the knife just as Haslett began to raise his hand. A startled yell of pain left the young rancher's lips as the flying knife spiked into his hand.

"Gee, I'm sorry, Greg," Waco said, springing forward. "The danged thing just slipped out of my hand. Hey, cookie, you'd best take a look at this wound."

By tradition the cook on the trail or at a roundup camp acted as doctor for all minor injuries. The JA's cook, presiding at the fire, caught his cue and stepped forward.

"Dang fool trick to do," he said, taking Haslett's hand. "I'll have to bandage this up real good, Greg."

Stepping forward, the Flying M's cook gave a second opinion; and one which showed he read the situation right first glance.

"Sure needs doctoring up," he agreed. "It's sure lucky you wasn't aiming to use that hand for shooting or anything like that for a spell."

A look of baffled fury crossed Marwood's face as he saw the grins directed his way by the other men around the fire. He saw his chance of forcing a fight on Greg Haslett depart and turned his anger on the man who came between them.

Waco stood clear of the other men, his right hand

thumb-hooked into his belt near the staghorn butt of his off-side Colt. There was something about the youngster which gave Marwood pause to think. During the previous day Marwood had pegged Waco as a dressed-up kid who wore two guns but relied on his friendship with Dusty Fog and Mark Counter to shield him from trouble. Now Marwood knew different. Young Waco might be, but he stood full grown and did not need any man's shelter when the chips went down.

"Haslett paying you to fight his fight?" Marwood asked.

"Didn't know he had any fight, 'cepting the one you've been trying to force on to him," Waco replied. "Let's say I just don't like a man who'd blind a steer."

"You're pushing, boy," Marwood warned.

"You want for me to spit in your face?"

Which same laid things on the line as neat and tidy as any man could ask for them to be placed. Waco knew that Marwood would be a danger to Haslett as long as he was around, so the young Texan aimed to see that Marwood did not stay around much longer.

A change seemed to come over Marwood. He grinned and shrugged his shoulders as he looked straight at Waco.

"Shucks, I wasn't but funning and I'm not after any fuss with you," he said in a friendly and disarming tone—and his right hand grabbed at the butt of its gun, closing on the grip to draw the weapon.

It was a smoothly done move, one which showed practice. Only Waco failed to be deceived. In a flickering blur of movement the right-side Colt flowed from Waco's holster and flame ripped from the five-and-a-half inch Artillery barrel as it slanted upwards. Caught between the eyes by Waco's .45 bullet, Marwood pitched over backwards, his gun falling from a lifeless hand.

CHAPTER TEN

A Message For Captain Fog

"I had to shoot to kill, Dusty. He was too fast for me to do it any other way."

Waco stood at Dusty Fog's side and watched men carrying off the body of the gunman. The witnesses to the shooting hovered in the background and at one side Greg Haslett was having his hand bandaged by the JA cook.

"Where were you when the shooting happened, Jesse?" Dusty asked, looking at the segundo of the Long Rail as he hurried up.

"I stopped off at the remuda, Dusty. Got a couple of sick horses and I wanted to see if they'd have to go back to the spread."

That was a fair enough excuse, for a segundo had to attend to the well-being of his ranch's stock even before he thought of filling his own belly with food.

"How'd you stand on this?" Dusty went on. "Marwood was one of your men."

"He's only been riding for us since just afore the roundup. Uncle John took him, Curly, Gordon, and Walker on just afore the word went out about starting the roundup. Don't reckon any of our crew'd take up for him."

"Huh huh. See they don't. Way I hear it, Marwood was hunting for trouble and found it. Do you want to ask anybody any questions?"

"Your word's good enough for me, Dusty."

"Thanks, Jesse. Take the men and start them on cutting the *petalta*," Dusty said, then turned to look at Haslett who walked towards him. "How's the hand, Greg?"

"Hurts a mite, but I figger I'm lucky to be able to hurt."

"Make you feel any better, you can stick a knife in me," grinned Waco.

"I'd rather shake your hand, Waco," Haslett answered. "Why d'you reckon he kept riding me? He was doing it all yesterday and today."

"He know you from any place before you came here?" asked Dusty.

"Not as I remember."

"Maybe he's just a boss-hater," Waco suggested.

"And maybe you should he down with the *petalta* flanking down calves for the branders," Dusty grunted. "Is there anybody who might want you dead for any reason, Greg?"

"Not that I know about."

"Anybody after your spread?"

"No—Hold it though, some eastern land company made me an offer through Lawyer Scales. That was a few days afore the roundup, I said 'no' and that seemed to be the end of the matter."

"What was the name of the company?"

Haslett screwed his face up in an effort to help his concentration. Then he gave a grin. "The Primary Land and Cattle Company, they had some address in Chicago but I can't remember it."

"Did anybody else get an offer do you know?" Waco asked, having ignored Dusty's suggestion that he went to work and accurately followed his amigo's line of thought.

"Sure, most of us did," Haslett replied. "It looked a reasonable enough price for an untried range. Now I've seen the gather on the southern section, I'm not so sure about it."

Turning, Dusty looked at Waco with a cold eye. "Thought you had work to do, boy," he growled.

"Was just now going, less'n there's something here for me to do."

"Tell Lon I want him. You can take his place on the branding irons."

"Why'd you reckon Marwood wanted to make trouble for me, Dusty?" Haslett asked, watching Waco head for the remudas. "Was it to do with that offer?"

"I don't know. There could be any number of reasons."

"And how about what he said about Rosie?"

"Forget it," Dusty advised. "You knew Rosie had worked in saloons when you married her. But you still took her and you ought to know if she's been all you wanted in a wife."

"She has, and more."

"Then say to hell with the past. It's the present and the future you have to worry about."

"You could be right," Haslett said with a relieved grin. "She's—"

"One thing's for sure," Dusty interrupted. "She's not working on this roundup and you are. Go lend a hand with cutting the herd."

"I'll do that, Dusty—and thanks."

Watching the rancher depart, Dusty gave a little grin. A man never knew what problems he might find himself handling when he took on as a roundup captain. Then the grin faded as Dusty thought back on various incidents over the past few days. Two ranchers had nearly been killed and men recently hired by Chisum were involved each time. That business with the four Flying M hands, that could have made trouble among the ranchers had it come off. Maybe somebody did not want the roundup to succeed. One thing was for sure, Dusty meant to see that the mysterious somebody did not get his way.

When the Kid arrived, Dusty gave him orders which sent him riding across the range. On his arrival in Goodnight, the Kid first went to the Wells Fargo office where he sent a telegraph message off, then he headed for the saloon to see if Candy knew anything about the mysterious drummer who almost caused trouble for the Flying M boys. Candy could tell him no more than she had the previous night. It appeared that the drummer just materialized for the time he was in the saloon and then disappeared completely.

Shortly after sending the Kid's message, the Wells Fargo clerk looked out of his office into the gathering darkness. Leaving the office by the rear door, he went to the back of the lawyer's house. A couple of sharp raps on the door brought Scales to it.

"The Ysabel Kid just sent this off for Cap'n Fog," the clerk said. "You asked me to let you know if anybody sent anything to these fellers, or about them."

Taking the sheet of paper, Scales read the written message which had already been sent over the wires. His face showed no expression as he folded the paper and placed it in his pocket.

"I'll have to take it back for the files," the clerk said.

"Have you sent it?" growled Scales.

"Sure. I daren't hold a thing like it back."

With an angry snort, Scales returned the message form to the clerk. He looked down at the man's extended hand, gave another snort and dropped some money into the waiting palm.

He watched the clerk hurry away then turned and entered the house, locking the door behind him. Walking back to the living room, he entered and looked at his guest. It was Laura Naylor and she sat in one of the easy chairs looking completely at home.

"What was it?" she asked.

"Captain Fog's sent a telegraph message to a friend on the Chicago police. A detective lieutenant no less and at Headquarters, asking about the Primary Land and Cattle Company. Fog's learned about it far sooner than I thought he would."

"They're the people who want to buy our place, aren't they?"

"Only if they can get most of the surrounding range too."

Opening her bag, Laura took out a folded sheet of stiff paper and spread it on her lap.

"I brought Jim's insurance policy to show you," she said. "It does have that New Orleans' clause that you mentioned. Will it still be legal?"

"It would hold up in a Texas court. But you know what the clause means?"

"I do," she replied and there was defiance in her voice. "It means freedom and a chance of getting out of this damned country for me, as well as something to live on. After all, it's only shortening the inevitable."

"You're a heartless bitch, Laura," Scales said.

Rising, she put her arms around his neck and drew his face towards her own. "That's why we get on together, darling," she siad and kissed him. "You're sure you can arrange things?"

"I can. I'm only waiting for the time to be right."

"Why?"

"Because I want to make my own ends pay as well as yours," he answered.

Once more a knock came at the rear door. Releasing Laura, Scales left the room, walked along the passage and opened the door. He did not take a lamp with him and scowled at the dark shape outside.

"What're you doing here?" he asked.

"Marwood's dead," the shape replied. "He was all set to drop Haslett when that kid Waco cut in. Gordon nearly got Bunyon killed yesterday too, but it didn't come off."

A curse left Scales' lips. It seemed that those four Texans were spoiling all his plans. The telegraph message to Chicago meant he must move quicker than he previously intended. He had hoped for a week to give his men a chance to get rid of some of the ranchers. Now he had at most three days in which to act, to break up the roundup and cause the ranchers to think of selling their property. All the ranch owners were still alive and he knew the only way to split them up was to get rid of the man who held them together, the roundup captain, the Rio Hondo gun wizard, Dusty Fog.

Scales had already thought of a plan to remove Dusty Fog. Although he hoped for a week, he decided to put it into action the following day. Telling his visitor to return in an hour, Scales went back to the living room. One thing was for sure, the truth about the Primary Land and Cattle Company must not come out. With that knowledge, Scales prepared to make sure the news did not reach Goodnight City in time to be of any use to anybody.

Nothing of note happened for two days. Each day the hands rode out and scoured the range, clearing area after area. Daily the *petalta* was cut and the maverick bunch grew by leaps and bounds. Although Dusty had a careful watch kept on Curly, Gordon and Walker, they behaved in a normal manner and gave no sign of being anything other than members of the Long Rail crew.

The day's work had ended on the second evening after Marwood's death and Dusty came into camp with Mark. They had seen the night herds were in place and both wanted a meal.

"We'll move the camp tomorrow, Mark," Dusty said. "This section's cleared and it's time we went north."

"Sure. I'll finish cutting the *petalta* and bring up

the maverick gather," Mark replied.

"Be best. By the time you reach the new holding ground, we'll have a fresh *petalta* for you to work on."

Dusty looked across the camp to the place where he and his three *amigos* bedded down. A feeling of disappointment hit him for, while the Kid and Waco were there, he could see no sign of Candy. The girl came out each night so far with the other townsfolk and Dusty enjoyed her company. In fact he had an uneasy feeling that he might have delayed shifting camp longer than was necessary just so he could have the girl come out to visit him.

"There's a letter for you, Dusty," the Kid said, holding out a white envelope. "It's sure smells pretty."

"Where'd it come from?" asked Dusty, opening the envelope and taking out a single sheet of paper.

"Dunno," admitted the Kid. "It was on your bed roll when we came in. Cookie says nobody went near your gear while he was watching, but he wasn't watching all the time."

Spreading out the sheet of paper, Dusty looked down at it. The first thing which struck him was how the edges of the paper appeared to have been wet and then let dry. Next he caught the faint aroma of perfume and lifted the paper to his nose. The perfume was there all right and the writing looked feminine.

"Dustine," he read. "I couldn't face seeing you again until we meet somewhere in private and I confess to you. If you come to the old Peters' place on the edge of town tonight, I will tell you everything I know, including how you came to be elected roundup captain in the first place. Please, Dustine, for the sake of our friendship, tell nobody about this, but come at around midnight tonight. Candy."

After reading the message twice Dusty lowered it to his side. There was much about it which puzzled him, much which did not fit the nature of the Candy he knew. While he had felt since Sunday that the girl wanted to tell him something, he wondered why she chose such a roundabout way of doing it. She could just as easily have talked with him privately in her rooms above the Juno, or even while out at the roundup camp.

"Is it private, Dusty?" asked Mark, cutting in on Dusty's thoughts.

For a moment Dusty did not reply. Then he made a decision and handed the sheet of paper to Mark who read it. A low whistle left the blond's lips as he finished reading and he passed the letter on to the Kid.

"What do you reckon, Dusty?" Mark asked.

"I don't know. But I figger to find the answer at midnight."

"You're going then?" asked the Kid, passing the note on to Waco.

"Sure. I reckon I might learn something."

"You reckon Candy might be involved in something?" asked the Kid.

"If she is," Dusty replied, "she's got good reason for being. What is it, boy?"

Waco held the paper to his nostrils and was sniffing at it like a coonhound hitting old ring-tail's line on a warm summer night. A puzzled glint came into the tall youngster's eyes as he handed the letter back to Dusty.

"How many of us are riding with you, Dusty?" Waco inquired.

"None."

"None!"

Three voices repeated Dusty's one word answer and for a moment he thought he would have a mutiny on his hands.

"If Candy's in some trouble, she wants me there alone. So I'm going alone. I went against the letter in letting you three read it, so I'll play the rest of the game the way it asks me to play."

"It could be a trap, Dusty," observed the Kid.

"Could be, Lon," the small Texan admitted, "but

we'll sure as hell never know unless I go along there and spring it."

While Dusty's three *amigos* knew there was no point in arguing with him when his voice took on that determined note, they still aimed to make a damned good try. However, before they could make a start, there was an interruption.

"Hey, Cap'n!" yelled the JA cook, his voice bristling with indignation. "I don't make favorites. So happen you ain't here soon, you'll go hungry 'til morning. Everybody else's done fed."

The threat broke up the meeting without further discussion or objections. All four Texans were too busy eating their food to argue more and by the time they finished Dusty took steps to prevent further discussion. He gave orders for the ranch owners, straw bosses and cooks to be gathered. While his three *amigos* knew what his game was, they obeyed the command. Dusty told the men they would be moving their holding ground and made his arrangements for getting the maximum work out of the cowhands despite the move. Admiring grins creased the faces around him as the men saw a master's touch in operation. Some roundup captains would lose a half day's work when moving camp, but Dusty Fog sure did not aim to do so.

"That's a fair-sized gather of unbranded stuff we're holding, Cap'n," Chisum remarked when the general business of the meeting ended. "Do you figure on splitting it yet?"

"Not until Monday like I said," Dusty answered. "I know it takes men to hold it, but I reckon we can split a larger number easier than a few."

A general mutter of agreement rose from the other ranchers. However, Chisum did not appear to go along with the majority.

"Suppose something happens?"

"Such as?" asked Dusty.

"Suppose the gather stampeded? You know how

longhorns are, especially wild stuff that's never seen a man, like a lot of that maverick stuff is."

"That's a big suppose, Mr. Chisum."

"It could happen, Cap'n Fog."

"Which's why I've got a night herd on watch, to see nothing happens. We'll make the split on Monday."

"That suits us," Haslett stated and the other ranch owners rumbled their agreement.

With a grunt and a shrug, Chisum turned and walked away.

Watching the Cattle King go, Mark Counter felt both annoyed and irritated. Maybe Chisum had only been giving Dusty a friendly hint, passing on some of his considerable wisdom, and, give him his due; Chisum had few peers when it came to the handling of cattle. Yet if anything should go wrong and the gather scattered those other ranchers would remember Chisum's words and blame Dusty for the delay in regathering the scattered mavericks along with the possible loss of a good number of the wilder animals. A stampede was always possible when dealing with unstable, irrational critters like longhorns. The blond giant knew enough about the roundup captain's job on a multi-ranch gather like this to be aware it was no sinecure. If anything went wrong, or anybody felt he had not been treated fairly, the blame fell on the roundup captain and he was held responsible, Chisum's words would be remembered if the herd should he scattered before it could be split and might easily lose Dusty his post as roundup captain.

For the moment, however, all was going well and all the other ranchers had nothing but praise for Dusty's handling of the roundup so far. The meeting came to an end and the group separated to their own affairs, the straw bosses to warn their men about the move, the cooks to attend to their chores and the remainder made for their visitors from town.

Dusty looked around, hoping to see Candy. There

was no sign of the girl and he doubted if she would come out alone after dark. So he next looked for Scales, meaning to question the lawyer about the Primary Land and Cattle company. Although Scales had been out every other night, Dusty could see no sign of the lawyer.

The evening passed pleasantly enough, although it would be the last time most of the town folk would come out to the camp. When the holding ground changed, it would be too long a ride for folks to take at night unless they had a much better reason than merely wanting to visit.

By ten o'clock the last of the visitors had gone home and most of the hands rolled in their blankets. Dusty, Mark, the Kid and Waco sat around the JA fire after the other men slept. None of the quartet said much and the matter of the letter was not discussed until shortly after eleven. Coming to his feet, Dusty looked at the other three.

"Nobody comes with me," he said. "Take over, Mark."

"I'll do just that," Mark replied.

Dusty collected his paint from the JA remuda and saddled the big horse. The night hawk thought nothing of this, for he had become used to Dusty taking the paint when making his rounds of the night herd. Remembering Chisum's words, Dusty rode down to the *petalta* and the maverick gather first. He studied the cattle and decided they looked settled enough. The two night herds on the maverick gather said that the cattle had bedded easy enough and not even the regular bunch-quitters were trying to break away. Looking up at the sky, Dusty saw no sign of a storm, or even a high wind that might spook the herd. Then he gave a grin. Chisum must be getting at him. If he did not watch out, he'd be jumping at shadows next.

Swinging the paint away from the herd, Dusty rode off towards town. The night herd watched him go, then gave a shrug, decided it was not his business where

Cap'n Fog went and so carried on with his work.

The old Peters' place lay just outside the limits of Goodnight City, a small, one-roomed shack reputed by the local kids to be haunted since Ma and Pa Peters died in it on the same night. It remained empty, and looked gloomy enough for the kids to be right as Dusty rode through the night towards it. There was no sign of life either in the shack or among the clump of willows which bordered the stream behind it. However, it was near enough town for the writer of the letter to have walked out instead of coming by buggy.

Dismounting, Dusty loosened the paint's saddle girths and left the big stallion standing with trailing reins. Then the small Texan walked towards the front of the house. His every instinct warned him of danger and his hands were ready to reach for their guns.

Dusty shoved open the door, its hinges creaked loudly but there was no other sound from inside the building.

"You in there, Candy?" he asked.

A low sighing moan answered him. Drawing in a deep breath, Dusty stepped through the door. He sensed rather than saw the dark shape at the left of the door, and heard the faint hiss of something lashed from the right towards his head. The something, he figured it to be the barrel of a Colt, landed. It struck the top side of his Stetson, crushing the hat's crown down on the small Texan's head. However, Dusty had already been going down and he escaped the full force of the blow; not that anybody would have guessed it from the way he collapsed face down on the floor.

"Got the short-growed bastard," growled a muffled voice from the right of the door.

"Two of them," thought Dusty: which same was reasonable odds, given surprise on his side and his knowledge of ju-jitsu and karate to back his play.

"Let's work him over some," suggested another voice.

"Don't be loco," snarled the man on the left. "I don't want him marked up when they find him in the morning. Do what I told you and no more. Bring the rope."

Three of them, not two. Still it was not too bad at that. A tingle of anticipation ran through Dusty as he heard the voice of the man at the left of the door. The first two had been muffled, as if the men were wearing bandanas drawn up over the lower parts of their faces for masks. Not so the speaker on the right. His voice sounded familiar; like Chisum's voice only different, as if the Cattle King was trying to disguise it and not entirely succeeding. More than that, the speaker did not address the man at Dusty's right or that third yahoo. He spoke to another member of the party who Dusty had not yet located.

"You want the laudanum as well, Mr.—" began the fourth man, his voice coming from the far side but drawing closer.

"No names, you fool!" snarled the man at the left, chopping off the other's words viciously.

"He can't hear us."

"Don't take chances. Roll him over."

Feeling the man at his right grip his shoulder, Dusty lay limp and relaxed as if the blow had landed with full power. He allowed himself to be rolled on his back without giving any sign that he could have prevented the action. The man who turned him stood astride his body, a big, burly and bulky shape in range clothes as far as Dusty could see.

"Pass over the laudanum," the burly man said.

"Tie him first," replied the man at the left.

The words changed Dusty's plans. At first he planned to lie still in the hope of identifying his attackers or learning what they aimed to do. Now he could not do so. He had no intention of allowing the men to rope him and drug him with laudanum at least not without putting up a hell of a struggle.

CHAPTER ELEVEN

I'm Putting My Life In Your Hands, Dustine

Dusty gave no warning of what he aimed to do. His move came suddenly, changing from stillness to violent action in a blurring split-second. A startled curse left the bulky man's lips as he felt a couple of hands clamp hold of his ankles. In the same movement as he grabbed the man's ankles, Dusty bent his own knees and brought his leg through the man's. Then he drove up his feet, ramming them into the man's stomach and at the same moment hauled hard on the trapped ankles. The man gave what started to be a yell and ended as a startled croak as he had the wind driven from his lungs and went over backwards.

While Dusty took the men completely by surprise, that jasper at the left proved to be able to react swiftly. Even before the bulky man hit the floor, the man at the left sprang forward and drove his boot out to catch Dusty in the side. Pain knifed through Dusty and he started rolling the instant the kick landed. Just as he rolled, the man kicked again but the foot missed and this time Dusty was ready. Catching the man's ankle in his hands, Dusty lunged to his feet without losing his hold. He aimed to twist the man's foot and flip him over in a manner which would cause him to lose all interest in the proceedings for a spell.

Before Dusty could put the move into action fully, a fist smashed into his face. The third man had come into the attack and the fourth was springing forward. Instead of flipping the man, Dusty lost his hold but not before he sent his man staggering. Hitting the wall, Dusty prepared to deal with the new menace. Number three swung again, shooting out his left at Dusty's face. Only once again Dusty was ready. Bringing up his right arm, Dusty deflected the blow over his shoulder and in the same move kicked out with his right foot, Dusty aimed at the knee-cap but in the darkness he missed his mark; which might be accounted lucky for the receiver of the kick. Although the man did not catch a broken patella, he felt as if his shin had been snapped and he reeled back howling.

Leaping by his hurt pard, the fourth man hit Dusty, ripping the small Texan's cheek and sprawling him backwards. Dusty felt two arms clamp around him from behind, pinning his own arms down.

"Get him!" screeched the voice of the leader.

Two shapes started to come towards Dusty, although one limped badly; and the bulky jasper was getting ready to rise, sitting up, cursing and shaking his head. Dusty knew he must get himself free—and quickly. The man holding Dusty felt the surging power as the small Texan exerted his strength and started to force the encircling arms open. Taken by surprise, he had never expected such strength in so small a man, the leader felt his grip slipping. Before he could tighten, the man had made the mistake of allowing Dusty to get his right arm free. Whipping his free arm up and back Dusty caught the man behind him around the neck. A fist smashed into Dusty's face, another into his stomach as the fourth attacker came into range, the third man limping up. Dusty felt the salty taste of blood in his mouth. Then he bent his knees slightly and forced his back into the leader's body. Another blow landed on Dusty and he straightened his legs, bending his body forward to catapult the leader over his shoulder and full on to the other two men. All three went down in a yelling, cursing tangle.

A sound brought Dusty around to meet the attack of the bulky man. Only he turned a mite too late. Two huge hands clamped hold of Dusty's throat and the man lifted Dusty, driving the small Texan back to crash into the wall. The thumbs gouged into Dusty's wind-pipe and the force of his arrival against the wall almost jarred the wind from his body. Dusty knew there was no time to waste in getting the big feller off him. With his fingers extended and held together, thumb bent over his palm, Dusty used the *tegatana*, the handsword of karate. He chopped the edges of his two hands into the bulky man's body. With a lighter man, Dusty would have injured the kidneys and the force of the blow caused the bulky jasper to relax his hold a mite, but not to release it. Up went Dusty's hands, grabbing the man's shirt at the shoulders. Bending both his knees as he jumped, Dusty got his feet against the big man's thighs. The weight bowed the big feller over until Dusty's buttocks hit the floor close to the man's feet. Then Dusty pulled downwards with his arms and thrust up with his feet. He heard the big man yell, then the hold on his throat relaxed and the man sailed over to crash on to his back.

The fight raged on through the cabin, but Dusty knew it was only a matter of time before the four men got him. He had lost his guns, for not even Joe Gaylin's holsters would retain weapons in such strenuous exercise, so could not bring the matched Colts into action. Time after time Dusty had been in a position to settle one or another of the men either with a karate kick or blow, or a ju-jitsu lock, but was attacked by another of the quartet before he could bring off the trick to a successful conclusion.

All four of the men would be carrying marks from

his hard fists, powerful fingers and savage kicks, but Dusty was marked up himself. His ribs felt as if they were caved in and blood ran into his left eye, partially blinding him.

Then it happened! A boot caught Dusty in the stomach and he went down winded and helpless. Fingers dug into his hair, dragging him up and a fist smashed into his cheek. Limp as a rag doll, Dusty crashed against the wall of the cabin and everything went black.

"He's done!" gasped the leader, shoving the bulky man aside. "Tie him up, one of you. Quick!"

Before two of the men could move, a third spoke. He had been knocked down by Dusty and dragged himself to his feet by the window. A sound attracted his attention and he looked out.

"Somebody's coming, boss!" he said, speaking muffled although he no longer wore his bandana mask.

"How many?" asked the leader's voice.

"Two of 'em—Hell's fire! That white hoss, it's the Ysabel Kid's."

His words induced something like a panic in at least two of the party.

"The Kid!" croaked the burly man through smashed lips. "I'm getting out of here—and fast."

Which sentiments were echoed by the other two, for both knew the Kid's well-deserved reputation as a night-fighter. Tangle with a bull longhorn when afoot and suffering from a broken leg; wrestle with a grizzly bear with one hand tied behind your back; throw lit matches into open kegs of gun powder; laze around naked in the open during a Texas blue norther storm: foolish actions all and deadly, but none of them as foolish or deadly as fighting that silent-moving, black-dressed, part-Comanche Dog Soldier wraith in the dark. So, while their boss showed some inclination to stop and finish his work, not one of the three men intended to do so.

Snarling in rage, the leader dropped his hand to

his waist band. He intended to put a bullet into Dusty
before he left. Moral scruples did not hold his hand.
Only the fact that the man, like Dusty, had lost his
gun saved the small Texan's life. For a moment the
leader hesitated, then the pounding of feet and rapid
opening of the rear door warned him that his "loyal"
helpers were leaving. Turning, he followed them,
plunging into the willows behind the house and keeping going.

The Kid and Waco brought their horses to a sliding
halt by Dusty's paint and both left their saddles before
the big stallions stopped. They lit down with cocked
guns in their hands and raced towards the shack. Both
heard the sound of rapidly departing feet and wanted
to learn what had happened to Dusty.

While the Kid preferred his knife for close range
work, or the magnificent "One of a Thousand" Winchester when a firearm was called for, his tactical
sense told him the handier handling capabilities of the
thumb-busting old Dragoon would best serve his purpose at that moment.

"Dusty," the Kid called, his voice floating almost
ventriloquilly so an assailant would have been hard
to put to pinpoint his position.

On receiving no reply, the two young men flattened
themselves on either side of the door. The crashing
in the willows behind the cabin door died off in the
distance. The Kid stepped around and kicked open
the cabin door, going in and to the left, dropping to
one knee and holding his gun ready. An instant later
Waco had entered the room and gone to the right,
also dropping. They moved in the way Dusty taught
them and as trained lawmen would under the circumstances. Although they did not need the precautions,
neither man regretted taking them.

A low gasping moan came to their ears. The Kid's
eyes, almost cat-like in their ability to see in the dark,
picked out the shape huddled by the wall.

"Light a match, boy!" he hissed, moving forward and holstering his Dragoon.

In the glow of Waco's match the two Texans saw Dusty. His hat had gone, his shirt was torn open and blood ran down his face.

"Where'd they go?"

Never had the Kid heard such concentrated fury as filled Waco's voice. If ever Waco had been a killer it was at that moment. The Kid knew he must act fast or see the youngster go on the rampage.

"See to Dusty," the Kid snapped, gripping Waco's arm as the youngster swung towards the cabin door, "Do it, damn you, boy!"

Cold murder glowed in Waco's eyes, but the Kid retained his hold on the youngster's arm. Then the match flickered out and a low groan from Dusty brought Waco back to sanity.

"Go get the bastards, Lon," he hissed and dropped to his knees at Dusty's side.

"I know I'm good, boy, but even I can't track in the dark. Let's see to Dusty, shall we?"

Waco saw the wisdom of the Kid's words. Striking another match, he illuminated his injured pard. Dusty moved, coughs racking his body, but to their relief the other two saw no sign of blood as he coughed. Weakly the small Texan shook his head, then he tried to face the light and raise his hands.

"Easy, Dusty," the Kid said gently, holding the small Texan's wrists. "It's all right, *amigo*. Take it easy."

"L—Lon?" Dusty gasped.

"As ever there was. Who did it?"

"F—Four—of 'em—"

"Four," Waco breathed, striking another match. "And he held them off. Is anything bust?"

"I dunno," replied the Kid. "I hope not, we sure as hell can't see if there is with just matches."

"G—Get me—Candy—" Dusty put in.

Once more the anger blazed into Waco's voice as he said, "Did Candy—?"

"Don't talk, boy," interrupted the Kid. "Move!"

"If I thought—"

"Don't try thinking, boy, you'll tire yourself," drawled the Kid, but his voice held no sting. "Help me get Dusty up."

Between them Waco and the Kid helped Dusty to his feet. Each holding one of the small Texan's arms across their shoulders, they carried Dusty from the cabin and towards the waiting horses. Waco could foresee trouble in getting Dusty on to the back of the seventeen hand paint. However, the matter did not arise. Leaving Waco supporting Dusty, the Kid brought his big white stallion forward.

"Hope ole Blackie remembers that trick we used to do down on the Rio," he said and gave a command in deep-throated Comanche.

Apparently the stallion remembered the trick, for it bent its forelegs and sank down on to its knees. Often on the Rio Grande in his tempestuous youth the Kid needed to mount a wounded companion and the old Comanche trick came in very handy at such moments. Helping Dusty on to the white's saddle, the Kid steadied him as the horse rose. Once in the saddle Dusty's horseman instincts kept him there. Even so the Kid bounced on to the rump of the white and helped support the small Texan, while Waco rode his own paint and led Dusty's.

Only one upstairs window showed a light as the three Texans rode towards the closed, darkened and silent Juno Saloon. Swinging from the white, the Kid felt around until he gathered a handful of pebbles. He tossed a few of the pebbles up at the window, waited some ten seconds and tossed more. Just as he was about to throw the last lot a mite harder, the window's sash lifted and Candy, her hair wrapped in a towel and her body draped in a blue quilted dressing gown, looked out.

"Who is it?" she called.

"The Kid and Waco," replied the Kid. "We've got Dusty here. He's hurt."

"I'll be right down!"

Candy's head disappeared hurriedly as she gasped the words. A moment later the window went dark and for a time nothing happened. The Kid and Waco helped Dusty from the saddle and led him to the rear door. Light showed under the door and the sound of rapidly-moving bare feet approached it. Then the lock clicked and the door opened.

"Oh, my god!" Candy gasped. "Don't stand there. Get him in. Take him to my room. Does he need a doctor? Is he badly hurt—"

"Don't go woman on us, Candy gal!" the Kid snapped. "We'll want hot water and some clean white cloths."

"Go along the passage here, Waco, the end door on the left leads into our kitchen. The stove should still be alight and you'll find a pan and the pump. I have all the white cloths we'll need upstairs. What happened?"

"Let's talk later," answered the Kid. "Give me the lamp and lend a hand with Dusty, Candy. Can you manage, boy?"

"If my matches hold out," Waco replied, walking off down the passage.

Between them Candy and the Kid helped Dusty upstairs. Some of the girls, disturbed by the noise, peered out of their rooms but Candy chased them back in again. Then she and the Kid took Dusty into her rooms. Setting down the lamp on the table, the Kid looked inquiringly at Candy.

"Into the bedroom and to hell with the conventions," she said.

They set Dusty down on the girl's bed and Candy dropped beside him, her beautiful face showing its fear and concern for him. Dusty lay limp and still again, his chest rising and falling as he sucked in air.

Turning, the Kid left the bedroom and returned with the lamp. In its light Candy saw Dusty's condition and she gave a shuddering gasp.

"Dustine!" she moaned.

Opening his good eye, Dusty looked at the girl. Slowly he lifted a hand to put it lightly on her head, shaking her gently.

"Easy, gal." he said in a weak voice. "It's not all that bad."

"Wh—What happened?" she gasped, unfastening his bandana and removing it. "I had a letter from you telling me to wait in town for you, and you nev—"

"I didn't write it, Candy," Dusty answered. "It was a trick to keep you away from the camp tonight."

At that moment Waco arrived, having found hot water on the stove. He entered the bedroom carrying a bowl in his hands. Rising, Candy hurried to the dressing-table and opened a drawer to take out one of her underskirts. Borrowing the Kid's bowie knife, she slit the skirt into rags and started to clean the blood from Dusty's face.

"Go fetch Dusty's gear from the cabin, boy," the Kid ordered.

On his return, Waco carried Dusty's Stetson and four guns—Dusty's brace, a Cavalry Model Peacemaker and a short-barrelled Merwin & Hulbert Army Pocket revolver—a coil of rope, something white and frilly and a pair of women's stockings. He found Dusty sitting on the bed, stripped to the waist and cleaned up. Although Dusty's left eye was closed, his top lip swollen, there were a couple of small gashes on his face and his body showed a mottling of bruises, he seemed to be able to think rationally and had no more serious injuries. Candy had done a real good job of cleaning Dusty up, gaining even the Kid's grudging approval in the gentle, yet thorough way she performed the work.

"What's that, boy?" asked the Kid, nodding at Waco's burden.

"Found it all in the cabin," Waco replied. "Were a couple of good whisky bottles, one'd've been about half full but they'd got bust—"

The words trailed off as he saw Dusty swing his feet from the bed and try to rise.

"The herd!" Dusty said. "We've got to get back to the herd."

"Easy, Dusty," groaned the Kid. "You'd never make it, shape you're in."

"We've got to. That letter, it was a trick to get me here, to discredit me. We've got to get back to the herd."

Shooting out his hands, the Kid forced Dusty back on to the bed, "Damn it to hell, Dusty, lie still. You'd only be in the way and slow us down. Me'n'the boy'll go."

Dusty knew the Kid spoke the truth. In his present condition he would be a liability not an asset. However, he could see the idea behind getting him to the Peters' place and knew the danger both to his reputation and the roundup. Mark could handle things at that end, providing the Kid reached him in time.

"Get going, Lon," he said. "Waco, take my hoss and stable it at Colonel Charlie's place, then follow Lon."

"Yo!" Waco replied. "How about you?"

"I'll take care of him," Candy promised. "Lie there, Dustine, while I see the boys out."

After she had seen Dusty comfortable, Candy escorted the Kid and Waco from her rooms. She was gone much longer than necessary merely to see them out and returned with a tray in her hands, a pot of coffee, milk, sugar, cups and saucers on it. Setting the tray down on the bedside table, she looked at Dusty as he swung his feet away from the bed and sat up.

"How do you feel, Dustine?"

"I've felt better, but I reckon I'll live. Give me my hat, Candy, and I'll head back to the herd."

"You're not going anywhere in your condition,"

she stated definitely and bent to catch his right foot. Before he could make a move to stop her, she had drawn the boot off and tossed it aside.

"Candy!" Dusty snapped, trying to rise and finding her strong enough to give him an objection as she put her hands on his shoulders. "They plan to scatter the herd—"

"And you've three damned good friends to help stop them," she answered. "They know what's been planned. Waco told me as we went downstairs."

"I thought he had it worked out," Dusty said with a wry grin and relaxed.

The bed felt soft and good to his bruised and aching body and he offered no resistance as Candy drew off his other boot then unbuckled and removed his gunbelt. Taking Dusty's belt Candy laid it on the bedside table and slid the Colts into their holsters.

"You can't be sure that's what they mean to do," she said.

"Why else would they lure me to town. They figured to drug me with laudanum to keep me quiet all night and leave me still drugged in the morning, but stinking of whisky and with those stockings and frilly do-dads to prove what I'd been doing all night."

"But why?" Candy asked.

"To get me out of the roundup captain's chore. Should the gather have been scattered, the ranchers would want to know why I wasn't there to stop it. You can bet the feller who planned it had things fixed so I'd be found and you might be able to guess what the ranchers would say when they heard where and how I apparently spent the night."

"Colonel Charlie would believe your story," Candy pointed out.

"Which same he's not here, gal, and most of the others don't know me any too well. Besides, they wouldn't' be too willing to listen to excuses. A roundup captain's supposed to be around to deal with any trouble that comes along."

"Who attacked you, Dustine?"

"Like I said," Dusty answered. "I don't know for sure until I've looked at a few faces tomorrow. There's a smart man behind it, Candy gal, one who can make a plan. Like that letter you received, telling you I wanted you to wait in town. That was to stop you coming out to the roundup camp and hearing about your letter to me."

"My letter?" she gasped. "I didn't wr—"

Reaching into his pocket. Dusty took out the crumpled letter and handed it to the girl. She opened it, read the message and a puzzled frown came to her face. Then she sniffed at the paper, rose and went to where the stockings and frilly-legged drawers lay on the floor. After examining the garments, Candy turned back and walked towards Dusty, her face working with suppressed emotion.

"I never wrote this, Dustine. That's not my perfume and those aren't my dr—garments. I wear that style, but they aren't mine."

"So I knew—about the perfume," Dusty told her with as near a grin as he could manage.

"Then why did you come?"

"To find out why it had been sent."

"Did you learn anything?"

Dusty put a hand to his face and grinned wryly. "You might say that I did."

Gently Candy reached out and took his face in her hands. She kissed him lightly on the lips. The time had come, though long delayed, when she must open up and tell Dusty everything about herself. Much as she hated the thought, Candy intended to lay her cards upon the table; even if it meant losing Dusty's respect. Slowly she moved away from him, her hands dropped to her sides, then twisted together in her lap. Dusty lay back on the bed and watched the girl's face, reading the misery and trouble upon it.

"In a way the letter told the truth, Dustine," Candy said, her voice fighting to stay steady. "I do know something about how you came to be elected roundup captain."

If Candy hoped to jolt some show of emotion from Dusty, she failed. Not by a flicker of a muscle did his face show any change of expression. In a way it was worse than if he had scowled, frowned, done anything.

"You've been wanting to tell men about it for a spell now, haven't you?" he asked, reaching out to take her hands in his.

"Ye—Yes."

Tears welled in Candy's eyes and Dusty tried to draw her closer to him. She had just taken a bath when the Kid's stones attracted her, and her body smelled warm, clean and fresh.

"Come on now, honey," Dusty said gently. "Tell me all about it."

Sucking in a long breath, Candy looked at Dusty. "All right," she said. "I'll start from the beginning. And in doing so, I'm putting my life in your hands, Dustine."

CHAPTER TWELVE

Steel In The Night

"In the first place, Dustine," Candy said, sitting closer to Dusty as he lay back on her bed and held her hands in his, "my name isn't Candy Carde, it is Vivian Vanderlyne—"

"Way you're waiting, I should know the name," Dusty answered. "I'm sorry, but I don't."

"It's not surprising," Candy smiled. "I was never really big in the theater, although several reliable critics said I had promise. I worked in the Southern States mostly, playing the best houses, singing, dancing, acting in juvenile parts, and while I was in New Orleans I met Vance Cornwall."

This time Candy saw the name meant something to Dusty.

"Would he be any kin to Harwold Cornwall?"

"Harwold was Vance's elder brother," Candy answered. "Mind you, Dustine, I never know a thing about Harwold's criminal activities. All I knew was that Vance had charm, money, not that that bothered me, and treated me well. I thought, and still think, that we were in love. We had a little place just off Jackson Square, that used to be the old Place d'Armes in the French Creole quarter."

"I know New Orleans, though I haven't been there since the War," Dusty told her. "What happened?"*

"Vance used to keep some money and a black leather-bound book at our place, he used to call it his get-away money. I always thought it was a joke. One evening, I'd been appearing in a show, I came home expecting to find Vance waiting. I found him all right. As I entered the apartment, I heard a woman's voice in the bedroom. She was screaming something about no damned actress taking her husband. Then there was a shot. I ran into the bedroom and there was Vance lying on the floor, blood running from his head, and a good-looking woman a few years older than me stood over him, a gun in her hand. I think I must have fainted, for the next thing I knew I was lying by Vance's body, the gun in my hand. Just as I was getting to my feet, I heard somebody banging on the downstairs door. I went to the window and looked out, there were two policemen outside. That was when I panicked. There was Vance lying dead on the floor and only I in the room, for the woman had gone. I knew what would happen to me. You know New Orleans society, Dustine?"

"I know enough about it," he agreed.

"They would never have listened to me," Candy went on. "What was I? An actress, the mistress of a married member of their society."

Candy shuddered as she said the words and dropped her eyes to the bed, not daring to look at Dusty for fear of what he expected to see on his face as she reminded him of her indiscretion. Releasing her left hand, Dusty placed his palm under her chin and gently tilted her face to his. He kissed her lightly on the lips and then took her hand again.

"The past is over, Candy. What you did before we met doesn't count between you and I."

* Dusty's visit is told in *The Rebel Spy*.

"Thank you, Dustine," she answered, a tear trickling down her cheek. Then she made an effort and regained control of herself. "I decided to run and I want you to believe me when I say that I had almost reached the rear door before I gave a thought to the money Vance kept in the apartment. He always said I was to have it if anything happened to him. So I went to the hiding place and took it out. It was in a small carpetbag and—although I didn't discover this until later—the black book was there too. I got out the back way before the police came in and fled to the theater where a friend bought me some clothes and luggage, then smuggled me to the docks and on to a riverboat. It was not until I was on the boat and going up river that I learned the book contained a complete record with names and dates, of Harwold Cornwall's criminal activities."

Dusty let out a low whistle, for he had heard something of the criminal empire of Harwold Cornwall. If Candy still had the book, it was the equivalent of a bundle of fused dynamite.

"I'll bet that got Cornwall riled," he said.

"It did and still has," Candy replied. "I took a job in Memphis, I cut my hair and dyed it black, thought I might be safe, but Cornwall's men came looking for men and I got out of town. So it went on all the way up river. Wherever I tried to stop, Cornwall's men would find me. So I decided to leave the river and head west. For all of two years I've been running and about eight months ago I met Hugo Scales in Forth Worth. By that time my hair had grown long and I let it go blonde. After being black for so long, I thought they might overlook a blonde girl called Candy Carde, and I think it worked. Anyway, Scales came to me one night and made an offer, to come down to Goodnight and run the Juno, acting and letting it be believed that I was the place's owner. He said he had a client who recognized me and who would hand me over to the law if I didn't agree. So I agreed. At first, well until a few days ago, it was fine. I knew enough about the operation of a saloon to make the Juno pay, and I could get out before a crowd and entertain. That was the thing I missed most about being on the run, Dustine, not being able to go on to a stage and hear the people applauding my performance. I did go on at first and that was how Cornwall's men used to track me."

She paused and they sipped at their half-forgotten coffee for a moment.

"When did things start to go wrong?"

"On the Friday before the roundup meeting. Scales came to see me, to check on the accounts as he did each week, or so I thought. When we'd finished the accounts, he said that his client—"

"Does this client have a name?" Dusty interrupted.

"Scales never mentioned it. He said his client which was how he always referred to whoever it was, wanted me to do something. He guessed the election of a roundup captain would be a tricky matter and cause a lot of argument. So he said I had to stand somewhere that allowed me to watch the northbound trail and when I saw a group of men, one of them wearing dark clothing and riding a white horse, come into sight I must go the ranchers and pretend to hurry them on. Then when they asked me to decide, I had to say that they might just as well take the first man to enter the main door as let me pick. I tried to argue, but Scales said his client would contact Cornwall and the local law unless I obeyed. So I obeyed, I couldn't believe that the plan would work—and I was scared and selfish enough not to want to lose the Juno."

"Most folks wouldn've acted the same way under the circumstances," Dusty told her. "And stop digging for sympathy or I'll kiss you."

Bending forward, Candy kissed Dusty lightly on the lips. "Darn those bunch. How can I give you a real kiss with your lip so swollen?" she said.

"Go on with your story," Dusty answered. "I'll chance a little pain later."

"Much to my surprise, the plan worked—to a point. Chisum was all against the idea and I think that turned most of the others for it."

"It sure would," agreed Dusty thinking of the way the other men acted around the Cattle King. "So they agreed—"

"And you walked in," Candy finished for him and then stared at him. "The plan must have gone wrong, Dustine."

"Why sure. Only I can't see any—Hey, Billy Bonney came in soon after we did; and he wears dark clothes and was riding a white gelding. It must have been him the affair was rigging to promote as roundup captain, but you made a mistake due to Lon's black clothes and that old Blackie horse of his."

"Bonney's a friend of Chisum," Candy pointed out. "Dustine, do you think Chisum is Scales' client?"

"One thing I learned early, Candy gal," Dusty answered. "Never make wild guesses or toss accusations around without proof. All I know is that if they'd got Bonney in as roundup captain this whole she-bang would have wound up in powdersmoke."

"How do you mean?"

"Bonney would have tried to help Chisum rob the others blind, and I can't see them standing for it. A range war, and one could have come out of Bonney's handling of the roundup, would have ruined most of the ranchers; they're living on bank loans until after they get on their feet. Has Scales' client been in touch with you since the Friday?"

"Scales came to see me on Sunday. He said his client wanted me to use our friendship to persuade you to wreck the roundup. I refused—"

"I thought you would."

"Thank you again, Dustine, you're making me

feel—oh, I don't know, happy, sorry because I didn't tell you earlier."

"Reckon you've been trying for days."

"I have, Dustine, I have. But I couldn't summon enough courage. I was afraid I'd lose you."

Dusty drew the girl to him and held her in his arms, feeling the stifled sobs shaking her. Not until the spasm had gone did he release her and when she raised her face to him Candy had regained her self-control.

"Scales said his client wouldn't like any refusal and then he left."

"And your horse bolted when you got into the buggy that night," Dusty remarked. "What kind of feller is this Scales?"

"Pleasant spoken, shrewd, an Eastern man; but no fool."

"Which's how I pegged him. I maybe ought to go—"

Coming to her feet, Candy looked down at Dusty. Grim determination showed on her face and she removed the towel, shaking her long blonde hair free.

"The only place you're going tonight is to bed," she said. "Do you hear me, Dustine?"

"I hear you, gal."

Dusty's body craved for sleep, but he doubted if sleep would come while he had so much on his mind. One thing he did know, looking at the girl's face, he sure wasn't going to get out of that room without a real powerful argument—and he did not feel like arguing at that moment.

"How about you?" he asked.

"I'll get by," she replied and went to blow out the lamp.

The bed-springs creaked a few seconds later and silence fell on the room. For a time Dusty lay restlessly tossing about in the bed.

"I hope to hell that Lon made the herd," he said. "Maybe I ought—"

"Dustine!" Candy answered. "Can't you forget the herd?"

Not for almost a minute did Dusty reply, then he said, "Know something, Candy gal? I reckoned I might at that."

After leaving the Juno Saloon, the Ysabel Kid and Waco collected their waiting horses. Just as he swung into the white's saddle, the Kid gave a chuckle.

"Thought ole Dusty'd want to know why we went against his orders," he said. "He forgot that when he left Mark in charge, Mark could send us out off his own bat."

"Why sure," agreed Waco, eager to fix the blame where it belonged.

"Take Dusty's paint to Colonel Charlie's place for the night, boy," the Kid went on. "Then go and watch that cabin until dawn. Maybe them fellers'll come back for the gear they left. Even if they don't you can follow their sign and find out where they went after they lit a shuck out of the cabin."

"By cracky, Lon, I do surely believe you-all started thinking," grinned Waco. "Always knew you'd get around to doing it some day."

"One of us has to, boy," the Kid stated and started his horse moving.

At such a moment Waco would never think of questioning the Kid's right to give him orders. He could see the wisdom of the Kid's suggestion. Usually it would have been the Kid who handled the lonely vigil at the cabin; but on this occasion his talents were required urgently elsewhere. Being an honest young man, Waco admitted—if only to himself—that the Ysabel Kid would be far more able to handle things on the range.

"You reckon they did bring Dusty to town so they could scatter the herd and leave it so folks thought he'd been spending the night in the cabin with Candy?"

"Sure do," Waco answered. "All the sign points that way and that's how I read it. Why else would they take the trouble to bring Dusty to town, aiming to hawg-tie and drug him?"

The Kid had seen examples of the way Waco could work things out on previous occasions. Likely the boy was near enough right in his guess; but damn it, a feller hated to see a smart youngster start acting like a detective. Little did the Kid know it, but the time would soon come when Waco's fame as a detective went far over the land.*

"You're giving me the lousy end of the stick again," the youngster drawled as they approached their separation point.

"Why else do you reckon we bring you along with us?" asked the Kid, then a thought struck him. "Hey, are you-all toting that fancy silk bandana?"

"You don't reckon I'd leave it where you, Mark and Dusty could lay your cotton-picking hands on it?"

"That's showing real good sense, boy. Don't you reckon you'd loan it to me?"

"You don't reckon right," Waco stated firmly.

"Which same it's important, boy," the Kid answered quietly.

Although Waco prized his silk bandana—newly bought in Polveroso City just before they rode out on a chore—he took it from his saddlepouch and passed it to the Kid. However, Waco felt a few words of sage advice might not be uncalled for.

"You muss it up, Lon," he warned, "and, so help me, I'll pluck me a quarter-Comanche scalp barehanded, see if I don't."

"Sure, boy, and I'll help you do it," the Kid replied. "See you around. And don't let anybody wide-loop the cabin, will you?"

* Told in: *Sagebrush Sleuth, Arizona Ranger, Waco Rides In* and *The Drifter.*

Waco's reply was brief, concise—but hardly to the point. Grinning broadly, the Kid touched his white's flanks and started the horse heading across the range at a fast lope. Waco watched him go, then grinned and swung his paint towards Goodnight's town house, leading Dusty's stallion behind him. After tending to the two horses and leaving them in stalls at Goodnight's house's stable, the youngster went to the old cabin. He settled down as comfortably as he could manage to wait out the dark hours. When dawn came there was still no sign of Dusty's attackers returning. So Waco located their trail, proving that the Kid's tracking lessons had not been wasted. He found where three of the men took their horses and rode off across the range, but lost the walking fourth member's line on the main street of the town. On going to Goodnight's stable, Waco found both paints still in their stalls. He saddled his own horse, decided not to disturb Dusty, and headed for the roundup camp.

Which covers Waco's activities, now to return to the Kid's adventures.

A man did not spend most of his growing years as the Kid had without developing the instincts, caution and keen senses of a much-hunted Texas grey wolf. Long before he reached the herd, the Kid sensed danger, felt it in the air. He was still a long three-quarters of a mile from the holding ground when the big stallion halted without any signal from him, its proud head thrown back and nostrils testing the wind as it looked off to the right. Instantly the Kid became as alert and wild-looking as the big horse—which was tolerable alert and wild. Men were hiding somewhere up ahead and the wind-borne scent carried to the stallion, which had been trained to give warning of such things. Nor were the men those who rode the night herd; of that the Kid felt sure, for he had a Comanche's ability to carry a map of an area in his head and could say exactly where the *petalta* lay. Any other men who might be around at that hour of the night could not be up to any good.

Riding up on the men might prove to be dangerous, for even the white stallion made a noise as it moved. So the Kid dropped from his saddle and gave thought to his armament. Once again he decided against taking along the rifle. In the dark a man needed neither the magazine capacity nor longer range of the Winchester, any shooting he did would be at close range where the Dragoon could best handle it. With that thought in mind, the Kid left his rifle in the boot and faded off into the darkness. He left the white standing free, secure in the knowledge it would remain motionless until he returned or whistled it to him.

After moving forward for a couple of hundred yards, the Kid came to a halt. All aroung him the night lay dark and silent, it might have been deserted of life for all he could tell. However, the Kid knew of more than one way in which he could find the men located by his horse. Taking out Waco's prized silk bandana from his pocket, the Kid spread it upon the ground, then lay flat and placed an ear on the silk. He did not do so to keep his face clean. In some way the Kid did not understand, sound carried through the ground and a silk bandana magnified it.

In the distance the Kid could make out the sound of horses moving; it would be the night herd riding their circle around the sleeping cattle. Up to the right, about where Blackie pointed the Kid could hear maybe three more horses moving and a man shuffled his feet. The Kid ignored the sounds except to mark their position on his mental map. What interested him most was the fact that a man on foot was moving about in the direction of the cattle, but between them and the Kid's position. He could only be trouble. While a member of the night herd might leave his horse to relieve himself, he would not walk that far from the herd.

Fixing the direction of the sound, the Kid rose and picked up Waco's bandana. It would be more than he dare to do to forget it since the boy set such a store by it. With the long, raking, mile-eating stride of a buck Apache, the Kid glided across the range. The sleeping cattle were not more than a hundred yards away when the Kid located the man he sought. They were on top of a gentle, bush-dotted slope and a big, bulky man came backing through the bushes in the Kid's direction. One glance told the Kid that he had arrived not a moment too soon.

Even as the Kid watched, the bulky man came to a halt. The man appeared to be limping badly and he held out the thing between his hands. For a moment the Kid felt puzzled, then he recognized it as being a keg about the size as used for transporting twenty-five pounds of black powder. The man held the keg as if pouring its contents through a small hole and on to the ground. While the Kid watched, the man set down his keg on the ground and reached into his pocket.

The Kid saw the whole scheme in one single, shocking blur of instinct. This was the thing Dusty feared, the attempt at scattering the herd of cattle. The man had laid a train of black powder through the bushes, most likely with a fair pile of it at the far end. Unless confined, black powder would not explode — but it burned with a brilliant light. When the train lit, its flaring light would startle the cattle and send them running in wild stampede.

Rasping a match on his pants' seat, the man prepared to light the end of his powder train. Instantly the Kid sprang forward. A startled curse left the man's lips as he heard the Kid's forward rush. Still holding the flaring match, the man twisted around and dropped his hand towards his hip. Just as he thought of drawing his old Dragoon, the Kid realized that a shot, while ending the man, might accomplish the powder train's work at the same time.

Instead of to the walnut grips, the Kid's right hand went for an ivory hilt and the Bowie knife came clear of its sheath. Even faster than the bulky, familiar-looking shape moved the Kid drew his knife. His arm rose and steel glinted in the night as the knife, with its eleven-and-a-half-inch long, two-and-a-half-inch wide blade, flew through the air towards the mark. Finely tempered steel, with an edge sharper than many a barber's razor and carrying a needle pointed tip to open the way for it, crashed between the man's eyes. Such was the weight and balance of the knife, and the texture of its steel, that, aided by the Kid's skilled arm, it split the man's head open like a blow from a butcher's cleaver.

Although the man must have died instantly and with his gun only just clear of leather, the lit match fell from his hand on to the end of the powder train. A flicker of flame rose into the air. Down by the cattle one of the night herd gave a startled yell and headed his horse up the slope on the run. The Kid ignored the man. Springing forward, he scuffed his boot through the grass ahead of the flame, scattering the other grains.

"Who's up there?" yelled the approaching cowhand and a second voice lifted in a demand for information.

"That's it, you blasted fools!" the Kid thought, looking down to make sure no spark of flame remained to catch the train beyond where he scattered it, "go scare those other two jaspers off afore I can get to them."

Lifting his voice, he took an elementary precaution. "It's me, the Ysabel Kid, don't come too close."

"What's up, Kid?" asked the night herd, it was Rocky of the Flying M, halting his horse. "Hey, who's that down there?"

"I'll look in a minute," the Kid answered.

Moving slowly, he went along the black powder trail, scattering it. As he had guessed, there was a fair pile at the end of the train, enough to have started every head of cattle at the foot of the slope running. After spreading the powder out, the Kid walked back to Rocky. Come the morning dew, happen nobody start throwing matches around afore then, the powder would be made useless.

A second man sat his horse by Rocky, both waiting for the Kid to return. The black dressed Texan went to the still shape on the ground and struck a match. In the flickering light the three men looked down at the body of Curly of the Long Rail. His face showed the marks of having been in a fight; and the top of his head—Rocky reckoned to be a hard young feller, but the sight of Curly's head caused his stomach contents to bulge up into his throat and only an effort prevented them from gushing out of his mouth.

"It's Curly," said the second man unnecessarily. He was an older hand than Rocky, but not less affected by the sight if his voice be anything to go on.

"Sure is," agreed the Kid, extracting his Bowie knife and cleaning its blade on the dead man's shirt—it took more than the sight of a dead enemy's blood and brains to worry the Kid's Comanche-toughened stomach. "Reckon he aimed to brighten the night for us."

"Huh?" asked the uncomprehending older hand.

"Was all set to lay a lit match to a train of powder he'd put out; only I reckon I stopped him."

"Yeah," grunted the cowhand, not looking at the body. "I reckon you did at that."

The old hand knew better than waste time in asking questions, but Rocky had yet to learn the value of discretion.

"Why'd he do that?" he asked.

"Maybe reckoned things were too quiet around here," answered the Kid. "He had at least one pard with him. I aim to try to find that one."

"Need any help?" Rocky inquired, hoping for something to relieve the monotony of riding night herd.

"Nope, but the night herd does."

After giving forth that wisdom, the Kid let out a shrill whistle. Hooves drummed and the big white stallion came to its master's side. Gripping the saddlehorn, the Kid went astride his horse and looked at the two men.

"How about Curly?" asked the old hand.

"Leave him lie until morning, so's the ranchers can see what he died for," replied the Kid. "See you later."

"We'll be around," grunted the old hand. "Let's get back to the cattle, Rocky."

Although he tried the silk bandana trick twice at different points, the Kid could locate no sound to tell him where the two men might have gone. He started to make a circle of the holding ground in the hope of locating the men, for he had no desire to spend the rest of the night guarding against them. Just as he had about half completed his circle, the Kid heard a flurry of shots from the roundup camp.

Curly's two bosom pards, Gordon and Walker, waited for the successful conclusion of their boss's disrupted plan. Neither felt any too happy about their position, for Dusty Fog was alive and free and his pards might even now be looking for his attackers. Time ticked by and still there was no sign of the flickering flame which would stampede the gathered cattle and allow the three men to rejoin the other hands during the confusion, so preventing any suspicion from falling on them.

Suddenly shouts rang out down by the herd and hooves drummed. The sound alarmed both men and had certain implications which they could read with ease.

"They've seen Curly," Gordon stated, speaking awkwardly through a swollen jaw and smashed lips.

"No shooting," Walker answered. "He'd've been throwing lead if—"

The same thought struck both men.

"The Kid!" Gordon gasped. "It must be the Ysabel

Kid and his knife that stopped Curly shooting."

Walker was already mounting his horse.

"Let's make a circle and sneak into camp to collect our gear," Gordon suggested as they rode away, deserting Curly's horse. "That damned Dusty Fog marked us up and he'll know it was us who jumped him."

Having no better plan, and not wishing to desert his "thirty year gatherings", Walker followed Gordon's lead. The long Rail crew had their camp set up slightly clear of the other outfits, for Chisum's "warriors" did not get on with the cowhands. This separation had its advantages, for nobody could watch the coming and going of the "warriors", nor did their night hawk better than half-perform his duties.

Nobody challenged Gordon as he walked by the tail end of the Long Rail chuck wagon and into the light of their fire. He did not sneak in, but walked normally as would a man just come from his spell on night herd. To sneak in would have been more likely to waken the Long Rail men than did walking normally. Crossing to the place where his, Walker and Curly's bed rolls lay, Gordon bent down to collect his belongings. He heard a footstep behind him, but thought it must be Walker.

He was wrong!

"Bad night for riding, *hombre*," said a voice Gordon recognized.

Hand slapping at the butt of his gun, Gordon whirled to face the speaker, Mark Counter stood not twenty foot away and from his position must have been waiting at the other end of the wagon. Seeing Gordon's move, Mark was left with no alternative. His right hand dipped and the long barreled Cavalry Peacemaker slid from its holster, lifting to bellow even as Gordon's gun cleared leather. He saw dust kick up from Gordon's vest and, hit in the left breast by the heavy bullet, the thin gunman pitched backwards, then to the ground.

Instantly the entire camp was awake, men cursing,

sitting up, or reaching for their guns.

"Behind you, Mark!" Jesse Evans roared, rolling from his blankets and throwing bullets from his ivory butted Colt.

Mark turned, his gun slanting up ready for use, but he did not need it. Walker hung against the side of the wagon and his gun slipped from his hand as he slid down; his head a hideous mess where the bullets had torn through it.

"What happened Mark?" Evans asked, coming to his feet.

"I was making my rounds and found Curly, Gordon and Walker weren't here," Mark replied. "There's been a few things about them I didn't like and so I decided to stick around and see where they'd been. Reckon Walker must have come up behind me. Thanks, Jesse."

"Buy me a drink some time," Evans replied. "I haven't liked any of those three since the boss took them on. Where's Curly?"

The Ysabel Kid could have answered that question, but at the moment he was riding towards the camp.

Looking down at the body of the thin gunman, Mark shook his head. "Don't ask me. What I'd like to know is who marked up Gordon's face like this. He looks like he's been kicked by a knobhead mule."

CHAPTER THIRTEEN

Miss Carde Goes To War

At eight o'clock in the morning Candy Carde sat on the edge of her bed and looked down at the still sleeping Dusty Fog. From there her eyes roamed across the room and came to rest on the dressing table. The previous night she had placed the note which brought Dusty into town upon the dressing table and so rose to walk across the room. Her black silk nightdress clung to her body and emphasized the firm-fleshed curves under it. Without a thought for her appearance, Candy took up the note and read it, then she raised it to her nose and sniffed at it once more. The sound of Dusty stirring in the bed caused her to turn. She looked down at his fight-marked face and a grim frown came to her brow.

Making her decision, Candy pulled open the top drawer of the dressing table and took out a combination chemise and drawers outfit of the latest design. She peeled off the nightdress and stood naked for a moment, then slipped into the underwear. Deciding to dispense with stockings, she went to the closet and opened it to take out a pair of medium-heeled shoes. Instead of her usual working clothes, Candy donned a white blouse and buttoned its hem to the top of a plain black skirt. Then she put on her cloak, gave her hair a rapid comb and slipped a hat on. Throwing a kiss at the bed, she left the room, carrying the letter in her hand.

Meeting one of her girls in the passage, Candy paused long enough to give her orders.

"Tell Len to wake Captain Fog at nine o'clock," she said. "Len can take him breakfast up and ask him to loan Captain Fog a shirt. If the Captain asks for me, Len is to tell him that I've gone to see the writer of the letter."

"Will Cap'n Fog understand, Miss Candy?" asked the girl.

"I reckon he will," Candy said and turned to walk away, but a thought struck her. "Tell Len that Captain Fog's horse is stabled at Colonel Goodnight's place."

"Yes'm," the girl replied and watched Candy walk away, a puzzled expression coming to her face. "Hum!" she mused. "I wonder how Cap'n Fog lost his shirt? If it was me, I'd rather have Mark Counter."

So might Candy have thought on first impressions, but she had no cause for complaint or to be dissatisfied with her choice.

The sound of knocking on the door woke Dusty. He lay for a moment, trying to decide where he might be. Then memory came back and he moved, giving a muffled grunt of pain. Swinging his feet from the bed, he looked around. Candy's nightdress lay on the bed and Dusty picked it up. Now that was a fancy looking outfit, he would bet Candy looked sweeter than a barrel of molasses wearing it. With the thought come and gone, Dusty bundled up the nightdress and slid it out of sight.

"Come in," he called.

Len, the head bartender, was noted for his skill as a poker player; he needed all his skill to prevent his surprise showing as he entered Candy's room. Bringing the tray of breakfast things to the bed, he put it down, looking with frank interest at Dusty's face, but asking no questions about the battle-scars.

"The boss left word for me to wake you at nine, Cap'n," Len said, taking the shirt he had carried over his arm and placing it upon the bed. "Said for me to loan you one of my shirts, so I brought this'n. Will it do?"

"Do fine, thanks, Len. Where at's Candy now?"

"Left word to tell you she's gone to see the writer of the letter—"

"What?" barked Dusty. "Hell's fire, Len, hand me my pants, *pronto!"*

The urgency in Dusty's voice made Len jump into action and forget the unasked questions buzzing in his head. Taking the levis, Dusty drew them on and he wasted no time in donning the borrowed shirt and the rest of his clothes. Strapping on his gunbelt, Dusty headed for the door.

"What about your breakfast?" Len asked.

"You eat it. Where's my horse at?"

"Colonel Charlie's place."

"Thanks. How long ago did Candy leave?"

"Getting on for an hour back."

"Damn that crazy gal," thought Dusty as he limped downstairs. "Doesn't she know enough to keep her head out of a trap?"

With an hour's start, Candy would be beyond any stopping; and there was a call Dusty had to make first. For once in his life Dusty wished that his big paint stallion had a gentler nature, or that one of his friends was around. No stranger could saddle the paint, not without considerable danger to himself. So Dusty would have to make his call, then saddle his horse and ride after Candy.

Going to Scales' house, Dusty looked through the office window. All the signs pointed to the lawyer having left in a hurry. The safe door hung open and a few papers lay scattered on the floor. Dusty went around to the rear of the house and, after making sure nobody saw him, kicked open the back door to enter the building. As he expected, Scales had gone. In Scales' bedroom, Dusty found that the bed had not been slept in although the lawyer had laid upon it during the night. The closet and dressing-table drawers had all been emptied and Dusty found nothing to hint where the lawyer had gone. Just as he was about to leave, Dusty saw what appeared to be a bunch of human hair lying on the floor under the bed.

"A false beard," he said, leaving. "This's who the drummer in the bar was."

On his way to Goodnight's house Dusty called in at the livery barn. What he learned there told him the situation was not as bad as he at first imagined—it was a hell of a lot worse.

"Is everythi—" Laura Naylor began, throwing open the front door of her house. The words died away as she found her early morning caller was not who she expected. "What are you doing here?"

Laura, wearing a woolen dressing gown over her underwear, stared at Candy. Stepping forward, Candy made Laura back off until they were both in the house, then the blonde closed the door behind her.

"I came to see you," Candy replied.

"Not this morning," Laura snapped. "I'm not in the mood—"

"This isn't a social call, dearie," Candy interrupted, moving forward and causing Laura to step away until they stood by the ornament-decorated side-piece. "I came to see you about the letter you sent to Captain Fog."

"L—Letter?"

"This one," Candy answered, taking it from her pocket and tossing it on to the sidepiece's top. "Its edges are soaked in perfume to make Dusty sure it had come from me. Only it's not my kind of perfume, and it's more expensive than any of my girls could afford. So I got to thinking who I knew used this kind of perfume and guess who the answer came out."

"I really don't know wh—"

"Cut it out, Laura dear. You wrote the letter and I want to know why."

Hate and anger blazed in Laura's eyes as she pointed towards the door. "Get out!" she hissed. "Get out, or I'll call the hands and—"

"They're working the roundup," Candy pointed out. "And you don't have a cook. He quit on you last week, you haven't been able to hire another. There're only we girls here, Laura. Now let's have a little heart-to-heart talk."

"And if I don't feel like talking?"

The gentleness dropped from Candy's face and her voice went hard. "Get one thing, Naylor, I aim to have the truth out of you even if I have to tear every hair out of your head to get it. Which is it, do we talk, or roll around on the floor for a while first?"

Candy did not know what she expected Laura to do next. Maybe the brunette would start talking; she might make a run for the stairs and the safety of her bedroom; she might even grab for hair, although Candy doubted if the snooty Mrs. Naylor would indulge in anything so unladylike as brawling.

So Laura's action took Candy completely by surprise. Suddenly and without warning, the brunette drove her left fist into Candy's stomach. The blow came so unexpectedly that Candy was taken completely by surprise. With a croaking gasp, she doubled over. Catching up one of the ornaments from the side-piece top, Laura swung it on to Candy's head. Two things saved Candy from serious injury: her long hair being able to cushion some of the force; and the fact that the ornament was a hollow vase which broke on impact. However the blow still landed with enough force to drop the girl on to her hands and knees.

Pain twisted Candy's stomach and made her want to retch, while the floor of the room appeared to be pitching like the deck of a ship. The broken vase clattered down at her side and she heard Laura's feet pattering away from her. Clearly the brunette aimed to get out of it while the going was good. Then the footsteps returned to halt at Candy's side.

"So you're going to tear out my hair, are you?" Laura asked.

Candy heard a swishing sound and then she screamed as a hot, burning sensation knifed across her back. Collapsing forward on her stomach, Candy twisted her head to look up. Laura stood over her, and through the tears which clouded her pain-filled eyes Candy saw the quirt held by the brunette. There was an expression of rage and hate on the brunette's face which told Candy she must do something, or be cut to ribbons with the quirt.

Even as Laura raised the quirt to strike again, Candy rolled over towards the brunette, locking her arms around Laura's legs and pulling. Taken by surprise, Laura went over backwards, giving a startled squall and losing her hold of the quirt. An instant later Candy landed on top of Laura and when she came, she came fighting.

Neither girl had ever been involved in a physical fight with another woman, but some primeval instinct directed fingers on to her hair. Tearing and yanking at each other's hair, the two girls rolled over and over on the floor. For almost five minutes they turned over in a wild tangle of flailing arms and thrashing, waving legs. Now and then one or the other would try to get to her feet, only to be dragged down again. They tore at hair, lashed out wild blows, bit and scratched. A small coffee table disintegrated as the girls, on their knees at the time, lurched over and crashed on to it. Laura's shapely legs waved wildly, the black silk stockings bursting at the knees, while runs split their length and the suspender clips popped. Both girls lost their shoes, and Candy's blouse separated from her skirt waist, but neither gave a thought to anything more than trying to hurt the other as much as possible.

At last Laura managed to force herself to her feet, dragging Candy up after her. The brunette was scared and hurt, already the first flush of triumph had left her. While she did not object to hurting Candy, Laura had no wish to take punishment herself. Desperately she thrust the blonde away from her, then turned and staggered towards the stairs. Once in her room a bolted door would keep her safe until help arrived.

Catching her balance, Candy shoved her hair out of her eyes and then went after the brunette. Already Laura was mounting the stairs and Candy grabbed out to catch the skirt of the dressing gown. Finding her progress halted, Laura pulled free the dressing gown's cord and wriggled from its sleeves. Candy threw aside her trophy and grabbed again. This time she caught Laura by an ankle, gripped it in both hands and pulled. Laura lost her balance, falling forward on to her face. Scrabbling with her fingers, she tried to prevent herself being hauled down the stairs. When that failed, she twisted around to try to kick at the gasping, pulling blonde. Taking her opportunity, Candy caught Laura's other leg. She braced herself and heaved hard, hauling the brunette bodily down the stairs. Staggering back, Candy sat down and Laura slid on to her, but before the brunette could make a move, Candy had rolled her over.

Once again the wild tangle raged across the floor. Candy's skirt ripped from hem to waist and her blouse lost a sleeve and was torn open before they came to their feet again. Not that Candy even thought about her appearance. Through the fiery haze which seemed to surround her, Candy was conscious of only two things; the slaps and occasional punches which rained on her face and shoulders, and the way she slapped and hit at the enraged face surrounded by a tangled mass of brown hair which floated before her. For a time the "splat!" of slaps, the crisper thud of punches, gasps, squeals and yelps of pain rang through the room. then the girls closed again, grabbing hair, scrabbling for holds on each other and both trying to bring the other down.

Candy shoved Laura backwards and ran at the brunette. Getting her hands against Candy, Laura pushed her away then grabbed up a plaster statuette from near at hand to hurl it at the blonde. Laura's downstairs main room was well-supplied with missiles and Candy caught up an ornament as the statuette hissed by her head. The air became filled with flying objects, statuettes, vases, ornaments, books, hurled with more or less accuracy. Although both girls scored hits, the matter was pure luck, not skilled aiming. Exhaustion welled through them and some of their throws barely reached half-way to the desired objective.

One throw landed. Caught on the forehead by a flying vase, Laura stumbled to one side and fell against the edge of the fireplace. Her hand felt something round, cold and hard, recognizing it as a steel poker. Even in her pain, rage and exhaustion Laura sensed the advantage the weapon gave her. She picked it up and reeled across the floor towards the other girl.

Gasping for breath, Candy leaned against the end of the sidepiece and stared at Laura. A realization of her danger seeped into Candy's head and just in time she thrust herself aside. Lashing down, the poker missed Candy's head by inches and laid a deep furrow in the sidepiece top. Staggering, Candy reached the bookcase which had supplied her with several missiles during the throwing session. One book caught her eye, a large, thick, leather-bound volume that looked mighty handy at such a moment. Drawing the volume out, Candy gripped it in both hands and turned to face her attacker.

Laura was no longer the elegant beauty who graced the dinner party. Instead of the supercilious smile, her sweat-soaked, bruised and bloody face bore a look of exhaustion but still latent rage, and was surrounded by a tangled mass of brown hair that had once been so neatly coiffeured; her magnificent body was bruised and sweating, clad in the tattered remnants of her underwear and one ruined stocking.

Not that Candy presented her usual attractive picture. Her long blonde hair resembled a dirty woolen mop and hung in front of her face; the blouse hung down, ripped away from her left shoulder and with the right sleeve torn off, her skirt still remained in place, although torn half off.

Swinging up the poker, Laura prepared to launch a blow at Candy. Only the blonde had raised the book and struck an instant ahead of Laura's move. Down came the heavy volume and thudded on to Laura's head. Dropping the poker, Laura staggered backwards. Her eyes were glazed and her legs wobbled under her. Letting the book fall, Candy stumbled after Laura and swung a round-house slap. Her fingers caught Laura's cheek—hard. The brunette spun around once more and fell face down on the floor, lying with her arms spread out and without a move.

Sobbing for breath, her body throbbing with the pain from various bruises and bites, Candy staggered forward, dropping to kneel by Laura and roll the brunette on to her back. Which was all Candy could manage to do for a time. She stayed on her hands and knees by Laura for almost half a minute, then managed to rise and headed for the kitchen. Pumping a bucket full of water, Candy sluiced her face and shoulders, trying to remove the sting of scratches. Memory of why she came to the Naylor place returned to Candy and she lifted the bucket. Reeling a little under its weight, Candy returned to the main room and halted by the groaning Laura's side. With an effort, Candy up-ended the bucket and tipped its contents over the other girl's head and body.

Gasping and sputtering, Laura came round under the deluge of cold water. Candy tossed the bucket aside and dropped to kneel astride Laura, getting a knee on each of the other girl's biceps to hold her even more firmly down.

"All right," Candy gasped, feeling Laura's weak struggles to get free. "Why did you send that letter?"

Only gasps and slightly more frenzied struggles answered the question. Three times Candy slapped Laura's face without any result. Then she dug her fingers into the brunette hair and started to pull with all her strength.

"Talk!" she hissed, pulling harder.

Squeals of pain burst from Laura's lips, then—

"I—it was H—Hugo Scales' idea!"

"Why did he want it written?"

"You'd better ask me that, Miss Carde, she doesn't know."

The voice, which Candy instantly recognized, came from the open front door behind the blonde. Twisting around, though still seated on Laura, Candy looked at the speaker's direction.

Scales stood just inside the door. Only it was a different man to the usual Scales who walked around Goodnight. He wore range clothes and had a Webley Bulldog revolver thrust into his levi's waistband; his face bore several bruises and he spoke through a swollen mouth.

"Get up," he ordered, walking forward. "This must have been some fight."

"Almost as good as the one you were in last night," Candy answered, forcing herself to her feet and ready to stop any attack Laura might make. However, the brunette made no move other than to turn on to her side and sob.

An admiring grin twisted Scales' face. "That's one helluva tough feller you have, Miss Carde. Damned if he didn't near whip all four of us. It's a pity I couldn't't've got him in with me. Get up, Laura; and stop whining, you aren't hurt that bad."

Slowly Laura lifted her head and looked at the man, then her face swung to Candy and hate turned it dark and ugly as she hissed, "Give me your gun, Hugo."

"Like hell. Go get cleaned up and dressed, we're getting out of here."

"But—"

"Do it damn you!" the lawyer roared.

Limping and holding her ribs and hip, Laura slunk towards the stairs and climbed them wearily. For a moment Scaled watched her go, then he turned to Candy.

"You'd best go in the kitchen and clean yourself up, Miss Carde. You're coming with us. I need more protection than Laura's presence will give me."

"Protection?" she asked, but obeyed, for some instinct warned her it would go hard unless she did as the lawyer said.

"Certainly. Why else do you think I'm taking Laura along?"

"I could think of a couple of reasons."

"That's pleasure, Miss Carde. I never mix it with business, except to the advantage of my business. And I wouldn't take a cold-blooded bitch like Laura for pleasure, that's for sure. Do you know her price for writing that letter?"

"No," Candy admitted, making for the sink and pumping water into a bowl.

"That I arranged the death of her husband."

"She wanted *that?*"

"She did. Laura hates Jim Naylor for bringing her out here and living instead of staying back east and dying of tuberculosis as a dutiful husband should. That was why she asked Captain Fog to tell her husband the ranch was a failure. She asked the night of the dinner, while you entertained her guests. Fog refused to go along with her, and she turned to me."

"I didn't know about that," Candy said.

"It's true enough. Anyhow, we discussed ways and means, and she mentioned that her husband's insurance policy carried a 'New Orleans' clause—"

"You mean the kind of thing that pays double indemnity if the holder is killed in a duel?" Candy asked. "I've heard of them, but I thought they weren't done any more."

"Some of the old-fashioned companies include them, although dueling is illegal. Laura wanted to know if the clause would hold water. Under certain circumstances, it would. So I arranged that Curly drew Jim into a quarrel over the tally book and shot him. Under Texas law, such a killing would class as an affair of honor."

"And she agreed to the idea?"

"My dear Miss Carde, Laura suggested it."

"Chisum picked a smart man to carry out his plans," she said, washing her hands and arms in the cold water and wincing as it stung a bite's mark.

As Candy hoped, the words struck a sore spot. Scales gave an angry snort and answered hotly, without thinking of the consequences.

"*Chisum!* He's nothing, Miss Carde."

"That's a powerful nothing," she sniffed disbelievingly.

"Did you ever hear of a stool bird?" asked the lawyer. "They used them on the East coast, captured wild geese that are staked out to attract other birds into the range of the guns. That's all Chisum is to me. Sure, he wanted to buy more land, and thought I was helping him. So I was, to a point. If anything went wrong, Chisum would have taken all the blame."

"That's easy to claim now," Candy answered.

"It's true. I work for the Primary Land and Cattle Company. They, the company, were indiscreet enough to sell shares in a ranch that would have taken in the entire Comanche range, before they bought the land.

Give them their due, they meant to buy this land, but those ten ranchers beat them to it. I was sent out here to get the land. Luckily the company did not have to declare a dividend for a year and there was still time for us to make good our claims to owning the land. Eight months ago I came west and established myself here. I did Chisum a small, tricky legal favor and realized he would be my ideal stool bird. When I suggested he put up the money for a saloon, he jumped at the chance. Only the two of us knew he financed the Juno and I looked around for a suitable owner. Marwood helped me. He recognized you in Fort Worth and I saw you would be the ideal owner, completely in my power."

"Then there was no 'client'?"

"Only me. Could you honestly see a blackmailer giving anybody his victim's secrets?"

"Not when you come to mention it. How did Marwood recognize me?"

"He'd worked for Harwold Cornwall, searching for you, the previous year. By the way, a six-months-old New Orleans newspaper reached me a couple of days back. The police have arrested Cornwall and broken up his gang. It seems that Mrs. Vance Cornwall got religion, confessed to killing her husband and blew the whole gang wide open."

"Then I'm in the clear?" Candy gasped.

"Only if Cornwall can be convicted on more than they have on him at the moment. And from what Marwood told me, you have, or had, the means to put a rope around Cornwall's neck."

"The book Vance kept?"

"Yes," Scales agreed. "Anyway, I brought you in to run the Juno—I must say you did a good job of it—and waited until we needed you. The chance came when the roundup meeting gathered. Only you picked the wrong man. I suppose that was an accident, wasn't it?"

"Was it?" Candy countered.

"Don't push your luck, Miss Carde," Scales warned. "You couldn't have even guessed—anyway, the plan went wrong, I knew Bonney would start trouble among the ranchers and a range war would have put most of them out of business and I could buy up the land— with everybody blaming Chisum for their trouble. When the idea failed, I told my men to watch their chances and get rid of the ranchers. I tried to stir up trouble through the Flying M boys in town, but the Kid must have stopped it."

"So you were the drummer?"

"And the cowhand who placed the burr under your horse's harness that Sunday," he admitted proudly. "I was always big in amateur dramatics in college and my disguises worked pretty well."

While Scales went on to confirm Dusty's theory for the letter, Candy finished her wash and managed to make her blouse look something respectable, although there was little she could do about her skirt.

"And now?" she asked.

"Now I'm getting out. I told Curly last night to report back after he scattered the cattle in an attempt to stir up trouble. He never came, so I assume that he, Gordon and Walker are either dead or running. If they'd been caught, they'd be talking their heads off and I'd have heard about it before now. I reckon I'll have a good head start, even if the ranchers don't blame Chisum for their troubles. But I'm taking you two along as insurance."

"Suppose I tear off all my clothes?" Candy asked. "You'd look a mite suspicious taking me then."

"I'd leave you—dead!"

From the matter of fact way that the lawyer spoke, Candy knew he would carry out his threat. Killing meant nothing to Scales, a life that stood in his way must he squashed out of existence as other men might crush a bug.

Before Candy could make any comment, Laura ran

into the kitchen. She wore an underskirt, but no dress, and looked both worried and scared.

"It's Dusty Fog!" she gasped. "He's coming towards the ranch."

Once again Scales showed how fast he could react. Even before Candy could do anything, the lawyer's left hand clamped hold of her wrist and his right drew the Webley to ram its stubnose into her ribs.

"Not a sound, Miss Carde!" he warned, shoving the girl ahead of him towards the kitchen door. "We're getting out of here and taking your buggy. I don't think Fog will follow us when he hears what I have to say."

Shoving Candy before him, Scales crossed the main room and went through the front door. A shock awaited him. He had been expecting Dusty to be a fair distance away and found the small Texan riding towards the house not thirty yards off.

Even as Candy opened her mouth to scream a warning, she saw Dusty's hands cross and read the indecision on his face. Then the Webley left her side and roared out. Dusty pitched out of his saddle, landing on the ground with a gun gripped in either hand.

"Dustine!" Candy screamed, struggling to free herself.

With a snarl of rage, Scales raised the Webley and brought it down on to the girl's head, stunning her. Yet he still held her on her feet and as a shield between himself and the still form of the small Texan as he shoved her towards the waiting buggy.

"Wait while I get a dress on and some of my things," Laura gasped, standing at the door.

Without lowering the dazed girl before him, Scales looked at Laura and gave a grin. "Sorry, Laura. Fog's friends won't be far behind and I haven't time to wait for you to dress. Besides, there's only room for two in the buggy and we can't wait to hitch yours. You'll have to stay on. Try poisoning Jim to get rid of him."

"Why you—!" Laura screamed.

She came at him like a wild animal. Twisting around, Scales shot her twice through the body—but in doing so he lost his hold on Candy's arm and the blonde staggered to one side, falling to the ground.

Guns thundered. Flame spurted from the matched Colts in Dusty Fog's hands. Lying on his stomach, blood tricking from the furrow carved by Scales' bullet across his neck, Dusty threw shot after shot into the lawyer. Reeling back under the impact of the lead, Scales tripped over Laura's body and crashed on to his back. Dusty came to his feet, saw that Scales still held the Webley and shot twice more. Having been a lawman, Dusty knew better than stop shooting when the other man was down but still held his gun—a thing Scales, for all his brilliance, had never learned.

"D—Dustine!" Candy gasped, staring at the small Texan as he walked forward.

"Keep back a moment, honey," he answered.

Going to where Laura and Scales lay, he looked down. Both were dead, but not until he was sure did Dusty holster his guns and turn to Candy.

"Dustine!" she cried, running forward into his arms. "I thought he'd killed you, Dustine."

"Not me, honey, I swore I wouldn't get killed until I saw you in that fancy black nightdress you had hid all last night."

Then he caught her in his arms as she slumped forward, and carried her into the house. Laying her on the settee, Dusty went into the kitchen and brought back a pitcher of water.

A short while later Candy recovered from her faint and lay looking up at Dusty. Bending down, he kissed her lightly on her swollen lip.

"Don't we look a mess?" he asked. "I do declare your shiner's bigger than mine."

It was then Candy remembered what Scales had told her. "Dustine," she said. "Mrs. Cornwall confessed to killing Vance, and the Cornwall gang have been arrested. I can go back and take up my career where I left i—"

The words died away as she realized what going back to her old career in the theater would mean.

CHAPTER FOURTEEN

I Want To Make You Happy

Dusty took Candy back to town and left her at the Juno Saloon while he saw the town marshal and told of the happenings at the Naylor place. An answer to the telegraph message Dusty had sent to Chicago brought confirmation to the small Texan's story. Before the marshall and Dusty rode out to the Naylor ranch, they called to see Candy and arranged that she send the incriminating book to the New Orleans authorities.

Although Dusty hoped to keep the true facts of Laura's death from Naylor, he could not manage to do so. Candy met the rancher and tried to convince him that the fight had been caused through her unfounded jealousy of Laura and Dusty, and that Laura died in a gallant attempt to save Candy and Dusty from Scales. The story fell through, for Naylor knew his wife's true nature too well; and, finding the letter, luring Dusty into town, recognized his wife's handwriting. At last there was nothing Dusty could do other than tell Naylor the truth, for the rancher was worrying himself sick trying to learn it. In a way Laura achieved her ambition. Naylor's health began to decline and a year later, having sold his ranch and moved further west, he died. So Laura had finally managed to kill her husband; but it did her no good, for she lay permanently under the ground of the country she had hated and feared.

A second ranch became vacant on the Comanche range, in fact it was vacated before Naylor left his spread. Two days after the death of Scales, Dusty returned to the roundup camp—Mark had assumed the duties of roundup captain in Dusty's absence and handled the work to everyone's satisfaction. On reaching the camp, Dusty sent word to Chisum that he wanted to see the Cattle King. Chisum had been expecting the summons and came prepared to use either his charm or bluff things out. Neither plan worked.

"You're clearing out of the Comanche range," Dusty said without preamble or mincing words. "I don't like range-hogs, Chisum. I know Uncle Charlie doesn't and I don't reckon the other gents are any too keen either. Don't insult my intelligence by pretending you don't know what I mean. I know the game you and Scales planned; only he was working for the Primary Land and Cattle Company—"

"You mean there is such a company?" Chisum growled.

"Until the Chicago police arrest its promoters," answered Dusty. "Scales worked for them, although if anything went wrong, it'd've been you who was blamed. And he knew Bonney wouldn't get things your way as roundup captain. The other ranchers would've fought first, which same would have broken most of them and let *him* buy their land dirt-cheap. I'll give you until we've gathered your stock off the Long Rail range—"

Which same was better than Chisum would have given a man in Dusty's position, but they saw things in a different light. Chisum had courage, no man could truthfully claim otherwise. Running a wild-onion crew like the Long Rail needed more than a sly knowledge of human nature, there were times when Chisum needed to stand firm and show his courage. Yet for all that, Chisum felt real, raw fear as he tried, and failed, to meet Dusty Fog's cold, grey-eyed stare.

"Miss Carde's going, too," Dusty went on when Chisum did not speak. "She's selling her saloon—"

This time Chisum was stung to make a reply. "I paid for that place."

"Can you prove it?"

The Cattle King's mouth dropped open and he looked like a fish out of water. There was no way he could prove his money paid for the Juno Saloon. Everybody around Goodnight believed, and he had encouraged the belief, that Candy Carde owned the Juno and he would have a hell of a chore proving different.

"But—but—" he spluttered.

"Like they always say," Dusty drawled. "Let the buyer beware. And one thing you'd best remember, Mr. Chisum."

"What's that?"

"Don't try to make any trouble for Candy. You couldn't hire enough 'warriors' to stop me taking you apart if you do."

"I'll mind your words, Cap'n Fog," Chisum answered. "Any time you want to change bosses—"

"That short of work I'll never be." Dusty said and brought the discussion to a close.

Watching Dusty walk away, Chisum grinned wryly. So he had lost a few thousand dollars and a fair strip of land, but he had come out of it alive and without losing too much face. The money could be regained from some other source and over in New Mexico there was much land to be had; good land—happen a man didn't mind fighting off Apaches and nesters—and land well clear of that soft-spoken *big* man from the Rio Hondo. Chisum had rarely been thwarted in his plans, he found the situation novel, but he promised himself he would stay clear of Dusty Fog in the future.

The roundup went on. Range after range was inspected by Dusty after his men scoured it and pronounced cleared. On the whole the gathers of cattle more than satisfied the ranchers—and the banker. Chisum's range, in fact the whole area, showed little stock with the Long Rail brand, but that was understandable; the Cattle King brought only a small herd in with him, expecting to grab off the lion's share of the mavericks to stock his land. Instead the unbranded animals, when shared, out, proved to be a sizeable bonus for the ranchers and one which ensured the continuance of even the poorest rancher.

Then one day, Tuesday of the fifth week, it was over. Everybody breathed sighs of relief and thought of the fun they intended to have in town, Dusty and Mark helped work out the cost each ranch owner must pay towards the running of the roundup; the hands received their pay; and by Friday they were in Goodnight beginning their spree.

On his arrival Dusty went to see Candy and found her in a quiet, worried mood.

"I've sold the Juno, Dustine," she said. "The new owners take over on Monday, and I'm letting Chisum have most of the sale price, but keeping the bank balance for myself."

"That sounds reasonable," he replied, taking her in his arms and kissing her. "What's the rest of it?"

"The book I sent proved useful, Cornwall and most of the top men of his gang have been convicted on the strength of it—"

"And?"

"My name's not connected with the affair—"

"And?"

Misery twisted Candy's face as she looked at Dusty. "I heard from the Bijou Theatre, they want me to go to work for them, as lead in a new show."

"What do you want to do?" Dusty asked.

"What do you want?" she countered.

"I want to make you happy, truly happy," Dusty

told her, "which same you never could be off the stage. Sure, I know you'd try—"

"If I was with you I could be happy."

"Sure, but I'd be away for months at a time. It's in my blood, riding with the floating outfit, just like going on a stage and listening to the applause is in yours. You'd never be happy while I was away, especially not knowing whether I'd make it back alive."

"You put it the way I feel," Candy breathed. "But I love you, Dustine."

"And I love you. Too damned much to tie you down. There's greatness in you, Candy Carde, and one day you'll be known throughout the world."

"But I'll never know another man like you," she answered, locking her arms around his neck. "Now kiss me and then let's go and get some money in the till."

Never would Goodnight City forget the celebrations of Friday and Saturday; and for once the local citizens did not mind the wild cowhand horseplay. Along towards midnight on the Saturday, Dusty and his three *amigos* helped the town marshal and Candy's workers, to clear the saloon. Candy whispered something in Dusty's ear as he helped Rocky of the Flying M from the room, then the girl went upstairs. When the last of the revelers had been escorted into the night air, Dusty left his friends and walked upstairs to Candy's room.

"In here," Candy called from the bedroom.

On entering, he found Candy waiting. She wore the black nightdress and, like he had figured, she looked as pretty as a June bug.

"When do you leave?" she asked.

"Monday morning."

"And me," she remarked, coming towards him. "We don't have a thing to do until then."

"Haven't we?" Dusty asked.

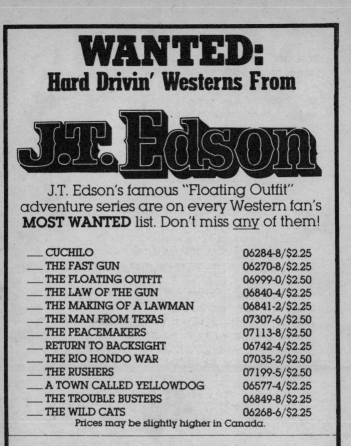

J.D. HARDIN

"THE MOST EXCITING WESTERN WRITER SINCE LOUIS L'AMOUR"
—JAKE LOGAN

____ 872-16840-9	BLOOD, SWEAT AND GOLD	$1.95
____ 872-16842-5	BLOODY SANDS	$1.95
____ 872-16882-4	BULLETS, BUZZARDS, BOXES OF PINE	$1.95
____ 872-16877-8	COLDHEARTED LADY	$1.95
____ 867-21101-0	DEATH FLOTILLA	$1.95
____ 872-16844-1	THE GOOD THE BAD AND THE DEADLY	$1.95
____ 867-21002-8	GUNFIRE AT SPANISH ROCK	$1.95
____ 872-16799-2	HARD CHAINS, SOFT WOMEN	$1.95
____ 872-16881-6	THE MAN WHO BIT SNAKES	$1.95
____ 872-16861-1	RAIDER'S GOLD	$1.95
____ 872-16767-4	RAIDER'S REVENGE	$1.95
____ 872-16839-5	SILVER TOMBSTONES	$1.95
____ 867-21133-4	SNAKE RIVER RESCUE	$1.95
____ 867-21039-7	SONS AND SINNERS	$1.95
____ 872-16869-7	THE SPIRIT AND THE FLESH	$1.95
____ 867-21226-8	BOBBIES, BAUBLES AND BLOOD	$2.25
____ 06572-3	DEATH LODE	$2.25
____ 06138-8	HELLFIRE HIDEAWAY	$2.25
____ 867-21178-4	THE LONE STAR MASSACRE	$2.25
____ 06380-1	THE FIREBRANDS	$2.25
____ 06410-7	DOWNRIVER TO HELL	$2.25
____ 06001-2	BIBLES, BULLETS AND BRIDES	$2.25
____ 06331-3	BLOODY TIME IN BLACKTOWER	$2.25
____ 06248-1	HANGMAN'S NOOSE	$2.25
____ 06337-2	THE MAN WITH NO FACE	$2.25
____ 06151-5	SASKATCHEWAN RISING	$2.25
____ 06412-3	BOUNTY HUNTER	$2.50
____ 06743-2	QUEENS OVER DEUCES	$2.50
____ 07017-4	LEAD LINED COFFINS	$2.50
____ 06845-5	SATAN'S BARGAIN	$2.50
____ 06850-1	THE WYOMING SPECIAL	$2.50
____ 07259-2	THE PECOS DOLLARS	$2.50
____ 07257-6	SAN JUAN SHOOTOUT	$2.50

Prices may be slightly higher in Canada.